Lethal
INCISION

A Dr. Zora Smyth Medical Thriller

DOBI CROSS

Luxhaven
Publishing

Interior Design by Luxhaven Publishing

Cover Design by Luxhaven Publishing

Editing by JD Book Services

To JC, Grandma D, and DC, whom I love more than life itself.

READ MORE BY DOBI CROSS

Dr. Zora Smyth Medical Thriller Series

Lethal Emergency (Prequel)

Lethal Dissection

Lethal Incision

Lethal Obsession

Lethal Reconciliation

Lethal Adhesion

SEE ALL OF DOBI CROSS BOOKS

at smarturl.it/DobiCross

AUTHOR'S NOTE

Thank you for choosing LETHAL INCISION. Zora Smyth was a character that I was fortunate to meet a couple of months ago as I brainstormed ideas for my first medical thriller story for an anthology.

LETHAL INCISION continues the story of Zora Smyth as she navigates life as a surgeon. She is happy with where her life is, yet the shadows from her past have caught up with her. We see how Zora is able to remain true to who she is, and how her compassion and love shines for those she holds dear.

It was important for me as I penned this series to have Zora Smyth not be some super hero or a person with extra ordinary abilities—she needed to be an every day person who just had unfortunate events happen to her. And who through the journey of the next few books comes to fully understand and appreciate who she truly is and is able to heal from the childhood baggage that she has carried all her life.

Please continue this journey with me in LETHAL OBSESSION. To order, please visit smarturl.it/DobiCross.

Would you also want to be notified when the next book in the series releases? Sign up at dobicross.com.

Once again, thank you so much for purchasing LETHAL INCISION and for meeting Zora Smyth. If you enjoyed it, please consider leaving a review at smarturl.it/DobiCross or recommending it to a friend.

Thank you again for your support!

Dobi Cross

Lethal

INCISION

A Dr. Zora Smyth Medical Thriller

The man stood still and watched the girl's eyes open and then widen as she looked down on herself. She was lying on an operating table, and sterile drapes covered her lower body. Her confused face was evidence enough that she had no idea how she'd gotten there. She tried to speak against the duct tape that sealed her lips, but all that came out was a moan which accompanied the *clink clank* sound which filled the air as she struggled against the metal restraints that held her down. But it was a futile exercise; he had soldered the metal cuffs to the table.

His eyes gleamed at the sight, and his breath quickened. She looked ethereal with her skin glistening with sweat—the sole artwork in a large room that was otherwise sterile white with bare walls. A recessed ceiling light washed over her, casting shadows over the rest of the space, even over the instrument table that stood next to where she lay. He sniffed the air and inhaled the scent of fear that radiated from her. The corners of his lips twitched upwards. Just the right combination, which meant she was ready for him.

He lingered for a moment on the scene before him, enjoying it before it would fade away never to reappear again. Then he stepped out from the shadows so she could see him. "Shh, relax," he said as he picked up a syringe filled with clear liquid from the open sterile pack that rested on the instrument table. "It won't take long. You want to be free, right?"

The girl managed a nod and the bouffant cap that covered her head slipped backwards to expose her blonde bangs.

"Good. And I will set you free, but maybe not in the way you expect." He chuckled against the surgical mask that covered his face. "But before then, you have to fulfill your end of the bargain."

The girl's brows creased into a frown, and her eyes blinked in rapid succession.

"Don't you remember? It's what you agreed to in the contract," he continued. He ran his gloved hand down her arm; it was soft and supple to touch. She had beautiful skin. It was a pity.

Her face turned ashen at his words. Her chin trembled, and the girl struggled to pull her arm away from him. But the restraint held it in place and instead left red marks around her wrist.

He brushed his fingers against the marks as if to smooth them. "It wouldn't have been this way if you hadn't tried to run away. And now you have to pay the price. You read the fine print, didn't you?"

The girl's eyes bulged, and her whole body trembled as what would happen next dawned on her.

This was the moment he loved the most. When their eyes registered shock, awareness, and horror at what was about to take place. And then the realization that they had brought it upon themselves. It was stupidity as far as he was concerned for them to assume that the terms of the contract would not be carried out. He chuckled again. "Now relax." He patted her arm. "I'll take care of you nice, quick, and easy." With no warning, he plunged the needle into her arm.

The girl jerked from the gurney as much as the restraints allowed, and a muffled cry rose from her throat.

The man discarded the empty syringe in the surgical bowl and waited for her body to slacken—usually took about three minutes for the drug to kick in. He'd timed it more times than he could count. Her body grew limp, though her eyes remained opened and stared out into space. Everything had been chosen for a reason: the injection site and the anesthetic drug of choice—he liked them to be somewhat dissociated but still awake, to feel pressure but no pain.

The man glanced at the clock on the wall. It was time. He'd already prepped her abdomen while waiting for her to wake up. So he picked up a scalpel from the instrument table. He would start with the left.

He slashed a four-inch midline incision down her abdomen instead of the more common flank incision. He could finish his work faster, and it wasn't like she was going to need this body in pristine condition where she was going. He switched to electrocautery and divided the subcutaneous tissue, muscles, fascial layers, extraperitoneal tissue, and the peritoneum. As usual, the ash-flavored tang from the electrocautery flirted on his lips. He ignored the taste and probed the tissues in the left upper quadrant of the abdomen with his gloved fingers till he reached what he was looking for.

Ah, precious commodity, ever smooth to the touch. He would have to be careful with it since it was already spoken for. He secured the blood supply, and then extracted the precious organ from the surrounding tissues that held it back. He lifted it from her body before placing it into the waiting receptacle. It was a cutting-edge organ transporter that hadn't been released to the market, and for which he had paid a premium. It suited his needs and had more than proved its worth since he started using it.

He took a quick look at the clock. He had about seven minutes left.

He turned back to the business at hand, reached into the right upper quadrant, and repeated the same procedure. The second organ went into an identical transporter. He sutured back the abdominal layers and then checked the time on the clock. He had managed to shave two minutes off his total time. An improvement, but he could still do better. He already had another idea in mind that he would try with the next case.

He knew without looking that the girl was dead. The second procedure had ensured that she would not survive. That was the punishment for trying to run away. It wasn't like he had forced her to sign the contract. It had been her choice, and she had been warned that she would pay a heavy price if she broke it. He'd gotten an extra organ to make up for the inconvenience of sending the boys after her. He probably could have taken more, but he was not a greedy man, and he liked to keep to the terms of the contract in question.

He wrinkled his nose at the pungent smell of

roasted flesh in the air. Time to clear it all out. He pressed a button on the wall. Erik, his bodyguard, would dispose of the girl's body, get the organs to their new owners, and ensure that the room was scrubbed down back to its pristine condition. He tossed off the surgical garb and dumped it with the gloves into a nearby chute. It led directly to an incinerator he had installed a couple of years ago for more effective waste disposal. He moved to the sink and scrubbed down his hands.

His phone buzzed an alert in his pocket. It was an alarm, reminding him of his next appointment.

It was time to head to the hospital.

2

T he beeping and hissing sound of the cardiac monitor filled the air in Trauma One like a time bomb counting down. A rapid sinus rhythm raced across its screen, the mirror of a desperate heart holding on for dear life. Zora Smyth, the fifth-year surgical resident-on-call for the night, took a quick scan of the patient—a young man, probably in his thirties, who lay on the gurney, still except for the rise and fall of his chest.

A narrow tube snaked from his mouth and was held in place with strips of tape. IV poles stood at a salute on either side of the patient's head, one line of Ringer's lactate running into a central line, the other into a vein on his arm. Bruises in explosive colors of red, black, and purple covered his face and torso in abstract patterns and created a colorful contrast against the EKG pads on his chest. His abdomen appeared slightly distended.

"What do we have here?" Zora asked as she grabbed a pair of gloves and snapped them on. Five sets of eyes looked back at her.

Thomas Stewart, the junior surgical resident-on-call, rubbed his bulbous nose before giving her a quick report. "Rick Williams, traveling with his pregnant wife, hit in a car accident by a drunk driver. Wife has been rushed to the labor room. Patient arrived unconscious to the ER.

"Pupils are equal and reactive, lungs are clear, but the abdomen is distended. There are no bowel sounds, and BP is seventy over thirty. Paracentesis showed blood in the abdomen. CT scan revealed a possible splenic rupture. Blood has been sent for STAT results and cross-match, and we are waiting for fresh blood and frozen plasma."

Zora put on her stethoscope to confirm what the resident said. The abdomen was quiet—silent like a grave. Not good. She checked his lungs; they were well ventilated, the endotracheal tube properly placed. She listened to his heart, which was barreling against the chest wall. Rapid sinus, but no murmurs. She replaced the stethoscope back on her neck. "Any medical history?" she asked.

"Wife confirmed there were no issues," Stewart responded.

A nurse called out. "V-fib! He's in V-fib! I can barely feel the pulse!"

Time seemed to pick up at a frantic pace.

Zora shot a glance at the monitor screen. The rhythm was rapid, unorganized, and barely discernible. "Start CPR. Stewart, you are in charge of the code."

Zora could see that the nurse had started pumping the patient's chest.

"We've got blood and frozen plasma!" someone called out.

"Let's hang them up," Zora said.

Fresh blood and plasma now replaced the Ringer's lactate dripping into the patient. Every drop and every second counted.

"Paddles ready?" Stewart asked. "One hundred joules."

Another nurse placed the defibrillator paddles on the chest. "Everyone step back!" she yelled.

The paddles discharged and the patient jerked off the gurney and back.

"Still in V-fib!" the first nurse responded. The air cackled with uncertainty.

"One milligram of epinephrine IV, then shock again at one hundred," Stewart called out.

The epinephrine slid through the central line. The torso jerked again at another shock of the paddles.

"Rhythm's back!" the first nurse shouted.

Zora checked the monitor. She would never get tired of seeing the sinus rhythm tracing advance across the screen. "What's the BP?"

"Seventy-five over forty." Good enough for now.

Zora took and released a deep breath. The aseptic smell of the hospital rushed into her nostrils, but she didn't gag. She was used to it. "Good job, everyone," she said, looking around the room as she removed her gloves. "But we are not out of the woods yet. Have we paged Dr. Edwards?" she asked Stewart. Dr. Chris Edwards was an associate professor of both Surgery and Oncology; he was the surgical attending-on-call and Zora's mentor.

"He's in the OR."

"Could you connect me to him?" Stewart strode off to summon Dr. Edwards, his average legs surprisingly eating up the distance to the nursing station.

Zora turned to the nurse standing next to her. "Do we have an open OR?"

"There isn't one available, and there won't be one

open for the next two hours, although …" The nurse exchanged a glance with her colleague on her left.

Zora drummed her fingers on the bedrail. "What is it?"

"Dr. Graham has an OR booked for a breast biopsy, but the patient is running late."

"Is there any reason why the surgery hasn't been rescheduled?"

"It's for a VIP patient."

Zora groaned inwardly. VIP patients were the most difficult to deal with. They made all kinds of demands and expected the medical staff to cater to their every whim. Elective surgeries were typically not scheduled in the evening. Zora was sure the VIP patient had requested it.

Everyone also knew that Dr. Ronald Graham could make your life more difficult. Zora and Graham were both chief residents, but Graham was the department chair's—Dr. Anderson's— lackey, and his pompous attitude didn't make him anymore likable. She couldn't afford to get on his bad side; it was the same as stepping on Dr. Anderson's toes, a risk she couldn't afford. This was her final year in the general surgery residency program, and she needed Dr. Anderson's sign-off to get a chance at the hospital's colorectal surgery fellowship. There was only one spot available, and Zora wanted it.

Lexinbridge was the only place she had ever called home, and she had no plans to leave anytime soon. She loved the town—a blend of the old with the new, with its charming colonial houses surrounded by modern edifices that radiated vitality and progress. Besides, she had gone to school here, and all her friends and family lived in the area. Yes, she definitely had to stay in town, which probably meant she had to remain in Dr. Anderson's good graces.

But Zora looked at Mr. Williams again. They had barely managed to stabilize him, and they needed to get him into the OR as soon as possible or he wouldn't have a fighting chance to live to see his first child. Cases like this always drew at Zora's heartstrings. She had grown up without a father when hers died in an accident, and she'd vowed to stop it from happening to anyone else if it was in her power to do so. She would regret it if she didn't do everything she could to save him. Even if it meant offending Graham.

She let out a deep sigh and looked at the nurse. "Do we have an ETA on when the VIP patient will be here?"

"I'm not sure, but unofficially, I've heard it might take the patient an hour-and-a-half to get here."

Zora rubbed her hand along her jaw. It would take about another thirty minutes for the VIP patient to be prepped for transfer to the OR, so she had about two hours. She could make it. She could be in and out of the operating room with enough time for OR turnover.

Zora turned to see that Stewart was back at her side, the top of his light brown hair sticking out in weird angles. Zora resisted an urge to pat it down.

"We are still trying to reach Dr. Edwards," he said. "The nurse-on-duty will let me know once she hears back from him."

"Okay. Which anesthesiologist is available?"

"Dr. Brennan is on-call. He just arrived," Stewart replied.

Zora liked Dr. Brennan. She had worked with him on multiple occasions and found him passionate about his work, yet very approachable. All the OR nurses loved him. He was the sort of person she needed in her corner to help this patient.

"Zora, I've got Dr. Edwards on the line," Christina called out. Christina was one of the ER nurses-on-duty and her best friend and current roommate. They'd been friends since high school, and Christina had moved in with her because Zora's mother was hesitant to let Zora live alone for medical school. And there had been no reason to move out since then. Christina had chosen a nursing career, training both as a trauma nurse and an OR nurse. It was always fun working with her in the same unit. And they were as different as night and day. Christina was petite with the most gorgeous red hair, while Zora was tall and curvy with curly dark hair.

Zora walked over to the nurses' station and mouthed a 'thanks' at Christina as she grabbed the phone receiver from her. "Dr. Edwards, we have a thirty-year-old male patient with blunt abdominal trauma from a car accident, and a suspected splenic rupture," Zora spoke into the receiver. "We need to get him into the OR for an emergency laparotomy. He's already coded once and we've stabilized him for now, but an OR won't be available for the next two hours. And I'm not sure he'll last that long.

"But Dr. Graham has an OR booked for a breast biopsy. It is open right now, and the patient is not expected to arrive in the next hour and a half. I can get this surgery done and be out before then. Dr. Brennan is the anesthesiologist-on-call, so we are in good hands."

The line was silent for a moment. Zora could hear the clanking of surgical instruments in the background. "Okay, let's get him into the OR. Tell the operating room manager I authorized it. I'm almost done with this surgery and will join you once I've finished."

Zora's shoulders relaxed. This was the reason why she loved having him as a mentor. Even though Zora had been inclined to think that Dr. Edwards would give the go-ahead—since it was always patients first with him—she hadn't been a hundred percent certain.

"Alright, thanks." Zora replaced the phone receiver.

"Let's get him into the OR," she told Christina.

She had a patient's life to save.

3

D rake Pierce folded his arms across his chest as he stared out of the floor-to-ceiling windows of his office. It was mid-morning, but he had been up for several hours already, his mind plagued—as it sometimes was—by the memorable incident that had occurred many years ago.

His face tightened as he remembered what had happened. He'd been a fool not to suspect Susie. But how could he have known that the number one H Club courtesan was the mother of Anna, the girl that everyone said he had raped? But it wasn't true. As far as he was concerned, it had been consensual, and she hadn't really protested. Why she'd chosen to take her life a few weeks later was still a mystery to him till this day. But all the blame had been pushed on him, and he'd been punished for it. Susie had ganged up with Alfred Pickles—Anna's father— to kidnap him. And Pickles had castrated Drake in the process.

Drake had fled the hospital the police had taken him to after they found him strapped on a table in the Gross Anatomy building. He'd gone into hiding and then turned around and meted out his own version of revenge. He never forgave anyone that crossed him. Susie was later found with her throat slit, and Drake put pressure on the police to close the case, though the killer was never found. Pickles was found dead in prison a few days later, killed by one of his fellow inmates. The police contact who had helped Pickles along the way died by accident on a hunting trip.

His lawyers had dealt with the rape charges filed against him. And they had delivered—the charges had been dropped after some time on a technicality, and the judge had agreed with it. Not that the judge had a choice—Drake's money had lined his pockets for many years.

Being a ladies' man, the castration had seemed like a death sentence for Drake, though his Adonis looks remained intact—sun-kissed wavy hair that comple-mented his piercing blue eyes and a chiseled symmet-rical jaw line that drew attention to a smile that the ladies loved. But he was lucky. The castration hadn't been total, and a top Spanish surgical team had performed a successful scrotum and testicular transplant. But it was not the same. He could never have biological children of his own.

The loss had also closed the door with Zora Smyth. She'd linked him with the rape case and had a hand in what befell him. So he'd passed judgement on her. If he, Drake, couldn't have her, then no one else could.

He'd kept tabs on her over the years through Tiny, his bodyguard. Somehow, he had become addicted to Tiny's weekly updates about her. And apart from a few dates she'd had with her investigator, Marcus Tate, she hadn't been with anyone else, which suited him just fine. She'd since blossomed into a gifted surgeon, while he, on the other hand, had been relegated to the shadows.

Drake's jaw muscle twitched. But he'd also lost one more thing. When the incident broke over the news, Drake's father had promptly disowned him and pushed him out of the Collmark Group. He had lost his position in the company though he had retained his shares —they were an inheritance from his late mother. Luckily, Drake had always had a contingency plan in place and had squirreled away a lot of money in offshore accounts. But he had become bitter toward his father—

he was shocked at how easily his father had tossed him aside and broken contact.

The new heir was his father's protégé: Steven Knox, a young man who had graduated with a PhD in Finance from MIT, his father's alma mater, and who sucked up to his father every chance he got. His old man's eyes must have been failing if he hadn't noticed the burning ambition in Steven's eyes. At that time, Drake had decided that if he couldn't inherit the company, then no one else would—the company was meant to be his. So he had spent the last few years secretly putting his plans into place.

The corners of Drake's lips twitched upward. One good thing had come out of the experience though—it had brought a new financial opportunity his way that would accelerate his long-term plans. He'd been approached through Tiny to invest in a certain kind of business, and it had since paid off in spades. And all he had been required to do was provide the cashflow—the rest had nothing to do with him.

And the business had an extra benefit.

It provided the perfect opportunity to rattle Zora's cage.

Forty-five minutes after Rick Williams' surgery, Zora walked out of the OR and made her way through the hallways to the call room. The surgery had been straightforward. She had ended up only removing the spleen; it had been severely damaged from multiple lacerations. Now, all they had to do was wait for him to regain consciousness. He'd been moved to the Recovery Room and would be transferred from there to the Surgical Intensive Care Unit, where the SICU team would monitor him closely.

Zora collapsed in one of the two chairs in the room and stretched out her legs in front of her. She removed the hair tie holding up her long curly dark hair in a ponytail and ran her fingers through her scalp. *Aah, this feels wonderful,* she thought. The call room was just good enough to unwind in, but too small for anything else. She looked down and saw the stains on her green scrubs. *Ugh.* Though Zora was used to the metallic cloying scent of blood, she didn't like to be around it any longer than necessary. She needed to change, but her body felt like jelly.

It had been a long day. Two appendectomies, one small bowel obstruction surgery, and one colon resection before this last surgery. Hopefully, the rest of the call would be easy. But that was the stuff of dreams. The ER was as unpredictable as a storm on the sea. Some days were quiet, while others were so chaotic that it was hard to catch her breath. She made a note to change her scrubs before attending to the next patient.

"Zora!" She looked up at the harsh sound of her name to see Graham standing before her, a Goliath on a mission, with his goatee-framed face looking ready to burst and his nostrils flared. His bald head seemed to pulsate. She hadn't heard him come in. "How could you take my spot?"

Zora sat up straight and sighed. She didn't really need this now. "Well, technically, I didn't take your spot. I just took advantage of an open OR and finished with enough time for it to be prepped for your patient."

Graham put his hands on his hips. "But that's not

the point, and you know it. You didn't even ask my permission."

Zora rubbed her forehead. "Sorry about that. I should have told you."

"That's it?"

Every word he spoke was like a hammer to her head. Zora massaged her temples. If only he could stop talking and leave her alone. "What else do you want me to say? I had Dr. Edwards' permission to make the change."

Graham pointed a shaky finger at her face. "Zora, you haven't heard the end of this." He turned and stormed out of the room.

Zora leaned back and closed her eyes. Finally, he was gone. She would have to face the music tomorrow, but that was okay.

For now, her body ached, and she needed some sleep.

A little after midnight, Zora's pager buzzed. She rubbed her eyes, but the sandpaper-like feeling behind her eyelids did not go away. She forced herself to sit upright, reach for the pager, and look at the screen. It was the ER.

Zora picked up the landline and called the ER nursing station. It was a patient with suspected abdominal bleeding. He had presented unconscious, with a roughly stitched gash on the right side of a taut abdomen. The ER team had already placed him on the ventilator, and he had an IV line connected to his forearm.

Zora twisted her hair into a bun as she made her way to the ER. She'd changed her scrubs as planned, but had ended up forgetting her hair tie. The area was so quiet that her footsteps echoed as she strode toward Trauma Two. Stewart was already waiting beside the patient, his thin lips in a frown as he stared at a CT scan film. He looked up and dropped the film back at the foot of the patient's bed when she stepped in and moved to the right side of the gurney. "What do we have here?" she asked Stewart. The patient appeared to be of Eastern European descent, with a physique that was no stranger to workouts.

"Patient is unconscious, but responsive to pain— there is abdominal tenderness, especially on the right upper quadrant. Lungs are clear and well perfused, BP is hundred over fifty, and the heart is in sinus rhythm. CT scan shows possible internal bleeding, but the liver appears normal."

"What's this? It seems someone has cut into this

abdomen before." Zora asked, pointing to the gash on the right side of the abdomen.

Stewart's nose twitched. "We don't know. The person who brought in the patient has disappeared."

Zora donned a pair of gloves and examined the area closely. She could see that the cut had been made with a surgical blade, but the stitching appeared amateurish. "This looks like the work of an amateur," she said. She peered closer at the wound. The epidermis over the area looked reddened and was slightly warm to the touch. She removed one of her gloves and checked the pulse on his wrist.

"Did we take a swab of this wound?" Zora asked Stewart.

"Yes, the ER nurse sent it to the lab. The STAT results should also be out soon."

"Anything else from the results we have so far?"

"The right kidney appears missing."

Zora's head swiveled in Stewart's direction. "Missing?" Zora grabbed the CT scan film and examined it. There was no mass where the kidney was supposed to be; the empty space was filled with a pooling of contrast material.

Zora's eyes widened. This was bad news. This patient needed an emergency laparotomy ASAP.

"Stewart, you should have told me about this first!

Page Dr. Edwards," Zora said. "Let's get John Doe to
the OR!"

———————

Zora woke up in the call room as the hazy light from
the rising sun peeked through the curtains and cast its
scattered rays on her face. She sat up, yawned, and then
stretched out her arms in front of and above her head.
She was sure her eyes were red. This was why she never
carried a mirror in her locker. Confirming the puffy
eyes and dark circles that she knew came with each call
would be pointless torture. She needed more sleep, but
she couldn't afford to dawdle. Today promised a full
schedule before she could leave for the day.

John Doe's surgery—they still had no name for the
patient—had ended well. They had drained a significant amount of blood from his abdomen, and Zora had
been able to find and cauterize the bleeders. The renal
blood supply had not been secured properly when the
kidney had been hacked out—hacked instead of
incised, because there was no way this was the work of a
surgeon. Otherwise, patients were in big trouble in the
hands of such a quack.

Dr. Brennan was supposed to have been on-call for
the surgery, but a different anesthesiologist had stepped

in for him. Zora had been disappointed. Given how many times they had worked together, she'd expected Dr. Brennan to give her a heads up if he wasn't going to be there. But he might have been held up in an emergency. She would check in with him to see if everything was okay.

Dr. Edwards hadn't made it to the OR as well, but the case had been simple enough for her to handle on her own. And she had kept him in the loop before and after the surgery. Zora had asked Stewart to follow the patient from the recovery room to the SICU. The rest of the night had been uneventful, nothing that she hadn't been able to handle.

Zora stepped into the adjoining closet-sized bathroom and took a quick shower. The cascading water soothed her skin and washed away some of her tiredness. It would suffice for now—she would take a full soak in the bathtub at home after the call.

She dried her hair and ran a comb through it before pulling it back into a ponytail. After donning a fresh set of scrubs, she put on her slip-ons and made her way to the SICU to get a head start on seeing all the patients she had admitted.

"I'm here to see John Doe," she told the SICU nurse at the central station, which was the primary hub for the twelve-bed closed SICU unit. Lexinbridge

Regional Hospital's SICU—manned by a collaborative, multidisciplinary team of health professionals—provided a high level of intensive care for over seven hundred critically ill surgical and trauma patients annually. These were patients that had either undergone highly complex surgical procedures or were very ill and required close monitoring. John Doe fell into the latter category.

"Give me one moment." The nurse typed into the computer in front of her. She tilted her head to the side and typed in some more. She looked back with a furrowed brow at the board behind her head.

"What is it?" Zora asked.

The nurse turned back at Zora. "There's no John Doe in the system," she said.

5

Z ora stared back at her in disbelief. "Are you sure?" she asked. "He was sent in here around two a.m. from the OR."

The nurse bristled. "Of course I'm sure. Look, he is not even on our board." She pointed to the digital whiteboard behind her head. "And if he is not in the system, that means no nurses or other members of the SICU team were assigned to him."

Zora stared at the list. There was no John Doe on it, though she could see the names of the other patients she had operated on. But there was no way he would have been transferred to the acute care general surgical unit without an initial twenty-four-hour monitoring period, since he'd been unconscious. Zora glanced around the unit, her mind racing for answers.

"What about Rick Williams?"

The nurse typed again into the terminal in front of her. "He is in N515." She clicked some more with the attached mouse. "Your other patients are also in the system. And as you can see, Rick's name is up there." She pointed to the whiteboard behind her again.

"Okay. Thanks. I'll take a look around to see if I can find him."

"Be my guest." The nurse turned back to what she had been doing.

Zora felt the eyes of the nurse on her back as she hurried through the SICU. *She probably thinks I'm cuckoo*, she thought. But Zora had operated on John Doe. That was the truth no matter what anyone said.

She looked into each rectangular cubicle. John Doe wasn't in any of them. She reached the end of the unit and turned back to check the other side. No John Doe. Zora leaned against the outside wall of the first cubicle and rubbed her forehead. What was going on? She'd never lost a patient before. And John Doe was not in a state where he could just walk off on his own. Unless someone took him away. But how was that possible without any discharge records? Zora would have been notified to sign off on it even if the discharge was against medical advice.

The missing records were more baffling. How could

that even happen? The Health Insurance Portability and Accountability Act of 1996, otherwise known as HIPAA, was a United States legislated privacy rule that protected individually identifiable health information held or transmitted by covered entities such as hospitals —patient records were sacrosanct, and measures had been put in place to ensure controlled access to the information. There was no way the records could have just disappeared.

Or had the SICU computer terminals malfunctioned? Zora shook her head. If that were the case, it would have affected other SICU patients, which meant the SICU nurses would be aware of the issue since they were each assigned to two patients at most per shift to ensure an effective twenty-four-hour monitoring of the patients. The nurse she had spoken to hadn't indicated that it was anything other than business as usual. And Zora's other patient records were just fine.

So what was really going on? Zora's head ached, and she rubbed her temples. This was not the best way to start the day. But where else could she check? The main medical records office was still closed, and it felt like overkill to go there anyway. And she still had to follow departmental protocol.

She would start at the beginning. Since John Doe

was admitted through the ER, there should be records there. Then there was her own operative report that she'd typed into the Electronic Health Records system. The anesthesiologist's inputs should be available too. Even the OR nurses would have their records as well. She'd also spoken to Dr. Edwards about the patient, and Stewart had been her first assist. So her first stop would be the ER, and then she would work through the list. If she hurried, maybe she could catch one of the medical staff she'd worked with overnight.

She straightened up and headed out of the SICU. Just outside its main entrance, she met the surgical attending intensivist and a senior anesthesiology resident—who had both been on-call—coming in to begin their morning round. Zora had worked with them before, so she knew who they were. She stopped to ask them about John Doe, but they both confirmed they'd been in the SICU for most of the call and hadn't met any John Doe either.

Zora rubbed the back of her neck. So where had John Doe been for most of their call? Stewart ought to know since he was supposed to have followed him to the SICU. So Zora called Stewart on her cellphone as she walked toward the elevators. The call rang through. "Strange," she muttered to herself. Stewart was still supposed to be on-call with her till eight a.m. She paged him and waited for his call back. No response.

She took the elevators down to the ground floor where the ER was located. The orchestrated madness called the ER—with its patients, family members, and hospital staff—gave off its unique cacophony as Zora walked in. She strode to one of the computer terminals at the central nursing station, accessed the system, and checked for her notes regarding John Doe. The search returned no results. She tried again to see if there were any reports linked to a John Doe. Nothing. No anesthesiologist's or OR nurses' reports. She turned to the nurse on duty who was working at another terminal.

"Hi, Mary. Could you help me pull up the records for John Doe that was admitted around midnight?

"John Doe? Let me check." She typed on the keyboard and straightened back up. "Hmmm."

'What is it? Did you find anything?"

"Nothing. There is no John Doe. Are you sure he was admitted yesternight?"

"This is crazy. How can a patient I operated on just disappear from the system?" Zora ran her hand over her hair. "Do you know if the anesthesiologists that were on call are still around?"

"You mean Dr. Brennan? He was the only one here, and he has left for the day."

"Wait, what? Wasn't there another anesthesiologist that stood in for him?"

Nurse Mary touched the base of her neck and frowned. "Dr. Brennan was the only one on the schedule, and he was here alone all night. You know how he likes to hang out in the ER."

"So you haven't seen the scrub nurses either?"

"What do you mean?"

"Never mind. Thanks, Mary."

"You're welcome." She turned back to what she had been working on.

Shaking her head, Zora pulled out her phone and called Dr. Edwards as she walked out of the ER. He should remember the patient. She had briefed him about John Doe before and after the surgery.

"Hi Dr. Edwards, I can't seem to find the John Doe patient I called you about this morning."

"Which John Doe?"

"The one with the missing kidney."

"I don't recall getting a call from you about such a patient."

Zora blinked rapidly. This was getting crazier by the moment.

"I did speak to you about him. I even checked in with you after the surgery," she insisted. "His medical records are gone."

"Zora, are you sure you are not mixing things up? The last patient I spoke to you about was the one with abdominal trauma." There was a pause on the other end of the line. "What about your first assist? Have you spoken to him?"

"Stewart? I can't reach him!"

"Calm down, Zora. If the surgery really took place, the operative report would be there."

"Sorry about that. This whole thing has been a little frustrating. There are no reports. All the records are gone. Dr. Brennan was the only one supposed to be on call last night, yet another anesthesiologist—who I had never seen before—stepped in for him for John Doe's surgery. And the scrub nurses were new."

"Look, Zora. Maybe you've been working really hard and just need to rest."

Zora stiffened. He didn't believe her. "I'm going to keep checking. If I don't find anything, I'll escalate it to Dr. Anderson."

"Zora, I'm not sure that's wise. Even though I gave you the go-ahead to take Graham's spot on the OR schedule—which I had every right to do—you and I know that he must have complained to Anderson by now. And Anderson is not going to let it go without finding a way to express his displeasure. There's no point in giving him ammunition that he can use against you, either to penalize you or even remove you from the program.

"Also, a missing patient record is a serious issue, and you need to make sure you have the evidence to back it up. From what you've said, there isn't any. And if this patient really existed, remember that it occurred on your watch. The question becomes how you let it happen. That's another mark against you. Why don't you wait till you have more proof? Hold on." Zora heard some muffled voices in the background. Dr. Edwards came back on. "Listen, I have to go. I need to take my wife to work. Let's talk when I get in."

"Okay," Zora responded. The call disconnected.

Zora closed her eyes and leaned against the wall. This was insane. A patient and his records missing? Zora still had a hard time believing it. There were checks and balances to ensure patient data safety. She couldn't fathom how this could have happened.

Her phone buzzed in her pocket. Zora retrieved it and looked at the screen. It was the alarm for her follow-up appointment with the oncologist.

She let out a long exhale. She had lost track of the time and had forgotten about the appointment at seven a.m. to review her yearly check-up results. Her stomach twisted into a knot, like it had done for the past eight years since she was first diagnosed. She hoped it was good news.

Zora sighed. She would first go for her appointment, then see to her other patients while still looking for John Doe.

She straightened and then headed to the second floor for her appointment.

"Dr. Smyth, how are you feeling?" The silver-haired doctor leaned forward, his elbows on the large cherry desk in front of him. Zora sat opposite him in one of two grey upholstered cherry-framed chairs facing the desk. The pale blue wall color was meant to give off a warm feeling, but it was lost on Zora. The cold tension from the threat of the cancer returning was more overpowering. Zora shivered.

"Are you cold?" he asked. "I can adjust the thermostat if you like."

"I'm fine." Zora gave him a small smile.

His pale blue eyes scrutinized her face. Zora could see the fatherly concern in them.

Dr. Braithwaite was the kind of man Zora wished her mother would date—he was tall, distinguished but very affable. And he'd been widowed for five years after losing his wife of twenty years. She'd grown to like him over the years since he'd become her oncologist. But every one of her attempts to hint at a potential date had been rebuffed.

"Really, I'm okay. What do you have for me, doc?" Zora asked. There was no point in beating about the bush.

Dr. Braithwaite looked at the screen of the computer perched at a corner of the desk. "Your results came out, and everything looks fine. There are no cancer cells, and you are still in remission."

Zora exhaled. She hadn't even realized she was holding her breath. The appearance of the acute lymphocytic leukemia eight years ago while she was a first-year medical student had been shocking to say the least. But Zora had been lucky. With a combination of chemotherapy and targeted drug therapy, and the support of one of the best oncology teams in the country, Zora had won the fight over cancer and gone into remission. She was a cancer survivor and was grateful for another chance at life.

"Are you still keeping up with your exercise and nutrition?" Dr. Braithwaite asked.

"Yes," Zora answered a little too quickly.

Dr. Braithwaite lifted an eyebrow at her. "Really? I recall a certain young lady that didn't like to exercise."

Zora laughed. "I still don't, but I've finally learned how to swim, which makes it so much easier to follow the exercise regimen."

"But?"

"Well, you know that the schedule of a surgical resident is crazy. I do the best that I can, which might mean missing a few days."

"Missing a day here or there is fine, but it shouldn't become a habit, Dr. Smyth."

"I know."

"Okay. Make sure you stick with the follow-up care plan with Dr. Wang, your primary care physician, like you've done all these years. Hopefully we'll continue to keep the cancer at bay."

"I'm on top of it."

"Good. So unless something happens or you suddenly start feeling tired again, I'll see you next year."

"Awesome." Zora gave him a broad smile. "So, have you been to the new restaurant three blocks away that opened last week?"

"Goodbye, Dr. Smyth."

Zora laughed. He was good at seeing through her attempts to set him up. But she wasn't going to give up.

Maybe one day he'd finally give in. She got up and left his office, shutting the door behind her.

Her phone buzzed in her pocket. Zora retrieved it and looked at the number. It was from the hospital. She swiped the green button.

"Dr. Smyth, Dr. Anderson would like to see you immediately," a familiar voice chimed.

6

"**D**r. Smyth, are you aware that you've violated policy?" Dr. Anderson's grey eyes bored into her from a bland face framed by curly wisps of alternating dark and grey hair. In another life, he could have passed off as a scientist. His bright red bow tie didn't help matters. He was a professor of Surgery and Urology with an endowed professorship in Gastrointestinal Surgery and had worked at Lexin-bridge Regional for many years.

Zora squirmed and fiddled with the gold pendant at her neck, which had been a gift from her late father. She sat opposite Dr. Anderson, a maple desk dividing them. But that was where the resemblance to Dr. Braithwaite's office ended. Books and medical journals overflowed from the shelves to the floor beside his desk and threatened to topple over each other.

Zora hated being in this position where she had to defend herself. "I understand this wasn't the best of circumstances, but a patient's life was at stake," she said. "The OR was empty, and I was in and out in no time. And I did get Dr. Edwards' approval to do so."

Dr. Anderson furrowed his brows. His curly hair moved as if to frown with him. "Dr. Smyth, I'm not sure you understand how serious this matter is. He leaned back in his chair. "There is a reason why we have policy. You can't just flaunt it whenever you choose."

"Dr. Anderson, I understand what you are saying, but that wasn't my intention. And I did try to follow departmental policy. It's been a goal for our department to minimize OR idle time. I tried to abide with that whilst saving a life. All the other ORs were busy, so I had no other option. And besides, Dr. Graham should have adjusted his block time with the OR operational manager once he knew the patient couldn't make it."

Oops. She could have done without that last remark. She really should learn to keep certain thoughts to herself.

Dr. Anderson glared at her. "Dr. Smyth, I believe you need more time to understand the gravity of the situation." He fiddled with a pen from his desk. "You'll be on-call for the next three days."

Zora groaned inwardly. Three days! She was just coming off a forty-eight-hour call and she needed her rest. But Zora didn't understand what that had to do with anything except … Her body stiffened as the implication dawned on her. The Gastrointestinal Conference. "But that means I won't be able to attend the GI conference in France!"

The conference was in three days. She had been looking forward to a relaxing time in France, and had planned to take two extra days off to sightsee before coming back to the States at the end of the weekend.

"Unfortunately, yes," Dr. Anderson intoned as if talking to a child. "I've already informed the organizers that Dr. Graham will be representing our department and attending on your behalf."

So this meeting had merely been a formality. Dr. Anderson had already made the decision before calling for her. Zora cursed Dr. Graham under her breath. He'd been vying for the spot and had been furious when the department recommended her. Now she had all but handed the opportunity to him. She took a deep breath and smoothed out the medical coat that covered her lap.

"I believe we are done here. Anything else?" Dr.

Anderson asked. He was already flipping open a medical journal that he had in front of him. Zora thought about mentioning the missing patient, but remembered Dr. Edwards' advice. She couldn't afford to make the situation worse than it already was. She would come back when she had more evidence.

Zora got up and shuffled out of his office. As she closed the door behind her, she bumped into Graham in front of the secretary's desk.

"Well, well, well, who do we have here?" he said. The smirk on his face made her want to dry heave, and she worked hard to unclench her fists.

But she could be civil. "Congratulations, I heard you stole my spot for the GI conference," Zora said.

"Correction. It was my spot originally. I just took back what belonged to me."

Zora's fists clenched up again, and it took more effort to relax them. The boxing ring was the only place where she'd have permission to smash the grin off his face, and Graham would never be caught dead there—he was a wimp at heart, despite how burly he looked.

Zora gave him a cold smile. This was not the time and place to get back at Graham. They had an audience: Julie, Dr. Anderson's secretary. And no matter how nice Julie was, she had loose lips that reported back everything she saw to Dr. Anderson.

And as angry as she was with Graham, she still had patients to see and a John Doe to find. Those were her immediate priority and what she had to focus all her energy on.

So Zora glared at him and stomped out of the front office.

7

Zora entered her apartment and dropped her honey-colored leather satchel on the grey granite kitchen countertop. She flipped the light switch on, and bright white light flooded the space. She had remodeled her apartment after graduating from medical school, and the magenta-colored kitchen with white cabinets and black granite countertop had been replaced by pale mint-green walls with contrasting rich natural wood grain cabinets and a grey granite countertop. Matching whiskey-colored bar stools completed the design.

But she was hardly around to enjoy it. The general surgical residency program had been hectic from day one, even though she'd loved every moment of it. She made it home just to sleep or take a soak in her claw-footed bathtub, which worked wonders in washing the tension and tiredness away. And she didn't see the routine changing anytime soon. In fact, her life might even get busier with the upcoming fellowship. It also accounted for why she was still single.

Zora had considered going steady a few years ago with Marcus Tate, her mother's favorite investigator. Her mother owned a law firm—Smyth Law Associates —and Marcus had worked full-time for her mother since after college and had risen through the ranks to become one of the lead investigators. Zora and Marcus had maintained a big-brother-little-sister relationship over the years, but an incident in Zora's first year in medical school had brought them closer.

She had almost been charged with the murder of a victim she'd discovered on her dissecting table as well as other murders the Formalin Killer had tried to pin on her. Marcus had been there throughout the ordeal and had helped her crack the case.

Zora had discovered Marcus was attracted to her, and they'd dated a few times. But she had kept their relationship platonic despite the crush she'd had on him before. Medical school and relationships did not mix well, and she didn't want anything to ruin their friendship. By the time she had graduated from medical school, their busy lives had taken them in different directions, and the possibility of a relationship was never raised again between them.

Zora shuffled into the living room and flopped down on the couch. She loved her color-splattered couch and had kept it during the remodeling, though the living room curtains now boasted a mint green and silver polka dot design set against pale dove-grey walls. Her green plants still hugged a corner of the room and looked like they needed some love. So she dragged herself from the couch and watered them with the little spray bottle she kept on her kitchen counter. Like her patients, she couldn't have them die at her hands. Once she was done, she plopped back on the couch, laid down, and closed her eyes.

The loss of the GI conference trip still irked her. It would have been perfect for her career. Not only would she have learned more about the latest breakthroughs in gastrointestinal surgery and the innovative techniques that surgeons in other parts of the world were experimenting with, it would have been a wonderful chance to network with some of the up-and-coming surgeons in this field, a great foundation for future collaborations.

She let out a long sigh. *I need to forget about this,* she thought. Easier said than done. But there would be more opportunities. She would make sure of it.

The sound of the Silent Night ringtone pierced the air. Christina had dared Zora to start Christmas early in the fall, and Zora had accepted the challenge. The Silent Night ringtone had been her response. She'd won the bet, but had decided to keep the ringtone all through till the end of the holidays. She still had a few more months to go.

Zora groaned. She didn't want to get up and hoped the caller would go away. Her body ached, and she needed a nap. She turned to her side and burrowed further into the couch.

The phone kept ringing. *Aargh.* Realizing that the caller wasn't going away till she answered, Zora sat up, shuffled over to the kitchen counter, and retrieved her phone from the satchel.

She looked at the screen. It was Adrianna Smyth, a.k.a. Mom. Zora hung her head. This was really not a good time. Zora's relationship with her mother had always been rocky since her younger sister disappeared, but only recently—after Zora had almost died at the hands of the Formalin Killer—had they grown close. They were still working out the kinks in their relationship slowly but surely. Her mother was still as busy as ever, but she now made some effort to connect with Zora on a regular basis. If she ignored it, her mother would keep calling and think something was wrong. Better to answer and get it over with.

She pressed the green button on her phone and held it against her ear. "Hello, Mom."

"Zora, how have you been?"

Zora leaned against the kitchen counter and pulled the hair tie off her hair with the other hand. "I'm good."

"You don't sound great."

"I'm okay. Just tired."

"How did your doctor's appointment go?"

She should have guessed her mother would keep tabs on it. "Only good news. Everything is fine."

She heard an audible sigh on the other line. "I'm glad. Anyway, I know you are busy and all. I just checked to make sure you're doing okay."

"I'm good. Thanks for asking."

"Okay, I'll talk to you later. I have a meeting starting in the next few minutes."

"Okay, bye." The line disconnected. Zora shook her head and chuckled as she ambled back to the couch, laid down, and closed her eyes. Her mother had not changed—she remained the queen of meetings. If Zora had a dollar for every time she heard her mother was headed to a meeting, she would have been a very rich woman by now.

Zora was no longer as affected as she used to be about her mother's penchant for meetings. It used to make her mad. But everything had changed when the pendant her mother had given her—a gift from her father, which her mother had modified to include a tracker—had literally saved her life. It seemed that was all she had needed—an assurance that her mother loved her. They still had some ways to go, but the relationship was getting better and better each year.

"Zora!"

Zora's eyes sprang open. She'd thought she was the only one at home.

"Zora, I didn't know you were back." Christina came into view wearing a pink T-shirt and grey yoga pants. Her gorgeous red hair was held up in a twist with chopsticks.

"Yep. I thought you were still in the hospital." Zora sat up to make room for Christina on the couch. Christina leaned back and placed her feet on the coffee table.

"My shift ended early. How was your day?" Christina asked.

"Hectic as always. But the weirdest thing happened to me today. My patient disappeared into thin air."

"Hmmm. Wait, what?" Christina sat up.

"Crazy, right? I remember operating on this one

guy—John Doe—and had Stewart follow him to the SICU. Now he's disappeared and there are no hospital records for him."

"And he wasn't discharged?"

"No. It's like he's never existed. Poof. Gone."

"How is that even possible?"

"That's what I've been racking my brain about. Dr. Edwards thinks I'm hallucinating."

Christina fixed her gorgeous green eyes on Zora. "Zora, if you recall operating on this patient, then you did. Don't let anyone tell you otherwise."

Zora gave her a hug. Christina's familiar soft lilac scent enveloped and warmed her. "That's why you are my best friend. Always in my corner."

Christina hugged her back. "Speaking of best friends, don't forget to buy me a gift in France."

Zora let her arms drop and leaned back on the couch. "The trip is cancelled."

"What do you mean cancelled? You've been looking forward to this trip for a few months now."

"I stepped on Graham's toes, and Dr. Anderson gave my spot to him."

"That's absolute nonsense! That toad. He's always after everything you have. So what are you going to do?"

"I have no choice than to suck it up. I now have to be on-call for the next three days."

"But you just finished your set of calls today!"

"That's Dr. Anderson's punishment for what happened. And I have to just accept it if I still want a chance at getting the GI fellowship. No sense in rocking the boat so to speak."

Christina's eyes searched Zora's face. "But are you okay?"

Zora allowed the corners of her lips to turn into a thin smile. "I'll be fine, eventually."

"I know what will make you feel better."

"What?"

Christina's face split into a grin. "Ice cream! I bought your favorite coffee flavor from the grocery store on my way back. Give me one second." Christina hopped up from the couch and headed into the kitchen.

The sound of Beethoven's *Fur Elise* filled the air. Christina pivoted and scrambled to her room.

Zora's face squeezed in concern. The only time Christina played classical music was when she was melancholic about not being in a relationship. Which meant she was more susceptible to accepting the next guy that came her way. That had resulted in some very terrible boyfriends in the past. Zora had even enlisted

Marcus' help to scare off one guy that had ended up stalking Christina. And the fact that she'd turned the music into a ringtone meant that Christina was feeling down in the dumps more than ever. This was dangerous.

Christina came back into the living room, a sheepish grin on her face. "Sorry," she said.

"Christina, what's going on?"

"Nothing."

"What do you mean nothing? You and I both know that you only play classical music when you're wishing you had a boyfriend. And now it's a ringtone?"

"Uhm, do you still want the ice cream?" Christina walked back to the kitchen and opened the freezer.

"Don't change the subject."

Christina turned and faced Zora. "Zora, I'm twenty-eight, and I don't have a boyfriend. Don't you think it's kind of pathetic?"

"Christina, the right person will come."

"Yeah, right. Like I haven't been waiting for like forever."

Zora got up and strode over to where Christina stood and held her by the shoulders. "You are gorgeous and stunning. The guys around us must be blind. Really, the right person will come."

Christina sighed. "Okay, but he'd better come soon."

"He will. Meanwhile, what's that?" Zora pointed at Christina's phone. A strange emoticon danced on the screen.

Christina's eyes followed Zora's gaze. "Oh, it's an alert."

"It looks creepy."

"I know. I've been using it to track my stocks. The market has been a bit volatile, so I've been more vigilant than usual about watching their performance."

"I thought you were careful about only investing in sound companies."

"I was. But something has been going on in the local stock market. There's been rumors in the online forums that it's being caused by the Collmark group."

Zora's other hand on Christina's shoulder fell to her side. She never thought she'd hear that name again. She leaned against the counter. "What do you mean?"

"The speculation is that Drake Pierce is behind it. Remember he had a falling out with his father after what happened? Word on the street is that the Collmark trades are destroying the value of their funds. There's no way his father would sabotage his own company. So that leaves Drake. He has the motive to do so, but a source at the company says there is no evidence."

Drake Pierce. The rapist who had been at the center of the storm that had almost ruined her life. If not for him, maybe Anna Hammond would have still been alive, and her father wouldn't have gone on a killing rampage. Which meant Zora wouldn't have been accused of being a murderer. "I thought they said he'd disappeared."

"Well, it seems like he's back. There's some speculation that he has been seen around town. So far, their funds have lost over a hundred million dollars. The trades seem to have Drake's fingerprints all over them, even though he's not supposed to still have authorization rights. First time it has ever happened to Collmark, but it's not looking good for them."

Zora shivered. She didn't want to dwell on the Collmark group, Drake Pierce, and what had happened many years ago. Besides, she already had too much stuff on her plate to deal with. John Doe for one. "Anyway, stay away from Collmark. We don't want to get entangled in their mess. Now pass me the ice cream."

8

C hristina sat on her queen-sized bed with her knees pulled up to her chin. She could hear Zora from the next room getting ready to turn in for the night. It was time for Christina to go to bed as well since she had a long day tomorrow. But she was worried about Zora.

When Zora had told her about the patient that had disappeared and the missing records, Christina had been shocked. As far as Christina was concerned, Zora's mental state was not in question. If she said a patient had disappeared, then the patient was missing. Zora had operated on John Doe.

Christina had never encountered this issue in all the years that she had worked at Lexinbridge Regional. Of course, there were patients who ran away from the hospital to avoid treatment or to avoid paying hospital bills, but missing medical records was a whole different issue. The hospital was fastidious about ensuring patient privacy, especially with the HIPAA law.

Which left only two options. Either someone had unauthorized access to protected health information, or a person at the highest levels in the hospital had authorized the deletion of the medical records. Either scenario had a lot of implications if the news leaked out.

Lexinbridge Regional would face civil penalties and damage to its reputation. Heads would roll, and some of those affected could even face criminal penalties and possible jail time. So either the culprit wasn't afraid of the consequences and was confident that the issue would not come to light, or he or she would be keen on covering it up at all costs. Whatever the option, Zora could be in danger if she kept probing into the case—she could be squashed like an ant that got in the way.

And Christina could not just sit on the sidelines and let that happen. Though she didn't have any tangible power or connections at the hospital, she was going to do all she could to protect Zora. Zora was the sister she'd never had. They understood each other and had stood together through thick and thin.

When Christina's mom had been very sick, Zora

had dropped everything to be by her side. Even dealing with Christina's relationship craziness was more than one person could handle, but Zora had never complained and always led the way in finding a solution to get Christina out unscathed each time. That was why Christina had been making an effort to get a strong handle on her relationship problem—Zora had no idea that the classical music ringtone was just a reminder to limit her urge to accept any boyfriend that came her way.

So when Zora had faced off with the formalin killer years ago, Christina had died a little inside, and the guilt was compounded by the fact that she'd been too busy at work to be there for Zora.

But this case was right on her home turf. And she was more familiar with hospital politics than Zora was. She wasn't going to stand by and watch Zora become the scapegoat if the case blew up. So she needed to keep an eye out on her behalf.

She closed her eyes and thought for a second. Maybe if she aligned her schedule with Zora's she could help in deflecting the coming storm. Because it was on its way. Christina sensed this was just the beginning.

Her nursing director owed her, and she would call in the favor tomorrow.

And maybe, just maybe, Zora would come out of it alright.

9

D rake closed the report he had been reading and tossed it on the right corner of his large mahogany desk. He looked up at a very muscular Tiny, who was standing before him in his usual black T-shirt over black pants, his jaw sprouting a new five o'clock shadow. "How much?" Drake asked him.

"Collmark has lost one hundred and twenty million dollars."

Drake rested his elbow on the desk and steepled his fingers. The amount was really a pittance compared to the ten billion in assets under management his father controlled, but it had made some ripple in the market so far. "Hmmm. That's still not enough."

"Should we continue?" Tiny asked.

"Yes, but make sure there is no evidence left behind. I'm sure those FBI folks are watching. They must have heard the rumors about my father and me. We don't want to give them anything they can use against us."

"Yes, sir. I have some guys watching over the team to make sure they stay in line. They know they are being compensated well enough to keep their mouth shut, and they are dead if they ever speak of it. We've also paid them in installments, so they can't go on a shopping spree and attract unnecessary attention to themselves."

"Good." Drake picked up his pen and opened the next report in front of him. When he sensed Tiny was still in the room, he looked up. "Anything else?"

"I got a message from your father. He wants to meet."

Drake stood up from his desk and walked over to one of the floor-to-ceiling windows that spanned half of his office wall. He stared outside at the twinkling lights from the building across the street. "That's not going to happen. It's not yet time. Ignore his message."

"Yes, sir."

"What about Zora?"

"She won't be attending the GI conference."

"How did she take it?"

"She didn't seem very happy about it."

Drake chuckled. He'd expected that. The Zora he knew would be pissed. As his plans unfolded, he was sure she would get more riled up. But if Zora was as good as he thought, the experience would only shake her up but not destroy her.

"Anything else?"

"None."

Drake swung his head around, his eyes observing Tiny's face. "Are you sure?"

Tiny didn't flinch and maintained his deadpan look. "Yes."

"Okay, you can go."

Drake watched as Tiny left the room. Why was Tiny lying to him? It was a good thing that he had another source, a guy who called himself Monkey—though Drake didn't understand why someone would give himself such a name—that gave him updates on all things Zora. Tiny had always been reliable, but Drake had chosen to be cautious instead, and it had paid off.

Monkey had reported that Zora had also lost a patient—a certain John Doe—and was searching everywhere for him. So why had Tiny excluded this news? Of course, Tiny had a crush on Zora even though he'd always tried to hide it from Drake—it had been fun taking advantage of this in the past. But still, he did everything Drake asked of him. So, what had changed?

Drake rubbed his jaw. The why didn't matter so much as the fact that he had done it. The only reason Tiny wasn't dead for this disobedience was because he was still useful. He'd just keep him out of his Zora Smyth plans for the meantime.

Drake ran his hands through his hair. His business was doing well, and he was making a ton of money. But he missed being at the center of Lexinbridge society. It had been too long. As much as he appreciated being in the shadows, he missed his old life. Maybe it was time to rectify that mistake. And it would also send the perfect signal to his father—he was available, but not to him.

It was time to visit the H Club.

10

It was a day later, and the ER had been relatively quiet. Zora yawned and stretched out her arms to shake away the fatigue. Dealing with the patients had run her ragged, and she really needed to sleep.

She was nowhere closer to finding John Doe. Every staff she had interacted with while treating him had claimed they couldn't recall him. She'd finally caught up with Stewart, and he'd drawn a blank on John Doe—as far as he was concerned they had only attended to Rick Williams, the abdominal trauma patient, but no John Doe. He claimed his phone was in silent mode the whole time she'd tried to reach him. Even Dr. Brennan had stared at her like she was nuts when she had asked about the other anesthesiologist.

Zora fiddled with the gold pendant around her neck. Was it true what they were implying—that everything was a figment of her imagination? It wasn't like she had post-traumatic stress disorder or anything—it had been years since the formalin killer case happened. But her memories of the patient and the surgery were so vivid that she was certain it had all happened.

She had to prove them wrong. If not, she would always wonder if something was wrong with her memory, and that would be a death sentence for a surgeon like her. The only way was to find evidence, but trying to track down John Doe, keeping up with her current patients, and being on-call at the same time had become a little too much for her. Her tank was running empty. Time to focus on something else for a change.

Zora logged into the hospital's system on the computer in the call room and accessed her department's training resources. There were some new minimally invasive surgery videos that she hadn't had time to study, and she picked one to watch. Minimally invasive surgery was another area of interest for her, her second choice subspecialty after colorectal surgery. In a perfect world she would be able to complete both fellowships, but that wasn't going to happen. Lexinbridge Regional didn't offer it that way. But Zora already had a workaround in mind that would allow her to get the best of both worlds.

Her pager buzzed. She unsnapped it from its hook on her waist and checked the message. She was needed in the ER. She took a deep breath and dragged herself up. She couldn't wait for this call to be over.

As Zora strode into the ER, someone bumped into her. Zora looked up to see a large framed muscular man dressed in all black with a snake-like tattoo peeking out above his shirt on the side of his neck. The guy glared at her and strode off.

Zora was at a loss for words. Who did this guy think he was? He'd been the one who hadn't looked at where he was going, and yet he'd had the audacity to be rude to her instead of apologizing. If she wasn't in such a hurry, she would have given him a piece of her mind. He was lucky that she had an emergency patient waiting for her care.

Zora arrived at the side of the patient's gurney just as the nurse was hanging up the IV line. The patient had been changed into a hospital gown and looked small on the bed with her arms restrained on the bedrail.

"Do we know why she is restrained?" Zora asked.

"She's been having mixed delirium—one minute

she is restless and hallucinating, the other she is quiet and withdrawn," the nurse responded.

"Okay, thanks." The nurse finished setting up the IV line and left the cubicle.

Zora looked at the girl's face. It seemed familiar, and her heart began to race. She moved in to take a closer look and gasped. The patient looked like her sister! It was the combination of the brown doe eyes, the small frame, and the honey-colored hair. Zora's hands shook and she gripped the bedrail. It had been a while since she'd thought of her sister. Not that she could ever forget her—the bright flame in her life that was suddenly snuffed out.

Zora took multiple deep breaths and relaxed her hands. She couldn't afford to go down this road now. The delirious girl lying on the gurney needed her.

She studied the girl's features further and noted that her facial bone structure looked a little different. More rounded at the jaw. It wasn't her sister. Even though it had been years since Zora saw her, her sister's face was a replica of her mother's, so it was easy to guess how she might look now.

The patient looked to be about nineteen years old. A quick glance at the monitor showed she had a respiratory rate of twenty-five breaths per minute, a systolic BP of ninety-five mmHg, and sinus rhythm.

Zora heard the sound of feet and turned. It was Charlie Newman, a fourth-year general surgical resident who was on call with her.

"What do we know about the patient?" Zora asked.

"Not much. No name." At Zora's surprised look, "She's been abandoned. A guy who claimed to be her brother brought her, but he disappeared before we could get her details. Big muscular dude with a sneer on his face."

The description matched the person who had bumped into her. "Did you notice anything else about him?"

"He had a tattoo at the side of his neck that was partly hidden."

It was definitely the guy she had met. "Hmmm. I wonder why he took off."

Zora checked the patient's pulse. It was elevated. Her olive skin was hot and clammy to the touch. Her abdomen stretched out like a semi-inflated balloon on her small frame.

"She's not pregnant," Charlie said. "We ran a pregnancy test before the CT scan. Her abdomen is taut with no bowel sounds. Paracentesis yielded blood."

Zora noticed an angry reddened slash with botched stitches on the left upper quadrant of her abdomen. She froze. Impossible. There was no way two patients could appear with missing kidneys within a few days of each other.

Alarm bells rang in her head. She grabbed the CT scan film from the foot of the bed and examined it. The left kidney appeared to be missing, but she couldn't be certain.

The hair on her neck rose, and she shivered. She felt the eyes of the resident on her.

"What do you think?" Zora asked him, her calm voice belying her the way she felt.

"Hypovolemic shock from a botched kidney removal, and possible splenic rupture complicated by sepsis. We've already sent the bloods for analysis and cross-match."

"We need to get her to the OR immediately."

The resident nodded and left to make the arrangements. Zora walked over to the nursing station and placed a call to the attending-on-duty. He was leading a complicated elective surgery that had extended into the night, but he gave Zora the go-ahead for the surgery and asked her to keep him updated.

Zora left the ER and made her way to the OR. As she scrubbed her right forearm with the brush in the pre-op section of the OR suite, Zora could not shake off the feeling that there was a connection between this patient and John Doe. Maybe there were other similarities she was missing. She sighed, switched the brush to her other hand, and scrubbed her left forearm. Just then, Graham walked in.

Zora's face froze. "What are you doing here?" Her voice sounded altered from the surgical mask she wore.

Graham refused to meet her eyes and walked to the other scrub sink. "I'm here to be your first assist. Charlie fell sick and had to go home."

She fixed a cold gaze at him. She didn't believe the story for a second—Charlie had looked fine in the ER. Something else was going on.

Zora finished scrubbing, rinsed her arm all the way to the elbow, and walked with her hands held up into the sterile section of the OR suite. The automatic doors opened with a swoosh. The anesthesiologist already sat at the patient's head. Bags of blood and frozen plasma hung on IV lines next to him and dripped life into the patient, and a systolic blood pressure of ninety mmHg registered on the monitor. He looked up, and she recognized him as the mystery anesthesiologist, the one who had worked on John Doe.

Zora felt her chest tighten, and she broke out in a sweat. The room seemed to close in on her. She stopped walking and took several deep breaths as she looked around the room. She didn't recognize any of the scrub nurses. It was like John Doe all over again. Then a certain nurse who had been busy with the instruments looked up at that moment.

Christina. Zora felt the white walls of the room recede. Her heart slowed its frantic pace. But what was Christina doing in the OR? Well, it didn't matter. She was just glad to have her in the room.

Christina smiled at her, and Zora nodded in return. With Christina around, there was no way this could be a repeat of the previous case. And if it was, at least she had a witness she could trust.

She turned to the anesthesiologist. "I don't think we've been introduced," she said.

"I'm Dr. Latam," the man said, his eyes boring into hers.

Zora studied him. "You were the anesthesiologist on the John Doe case."

The man said nothing, and instead turned to look at the screen of the monitor.

"Do you work here? I don't recall seeing your name on the on-call list," Zora pressed.

The blare from the monitor pierced the air.

"BP is crashing!" the anesthesiologist called out as he increased the flow of the fresh blood and frozen plasma into the IV lines.

Zora would have loved to question the anesthesiologist further, but she had a patient to save.

She strode to the patient's side. Graham was now in the room standing on the other side of the patient. She nodded to the rest of the team, passed her arms into the sleeves of the operating gown held out in front of her by a surgical tech, and allowed him to cover her hands with a pair of surgical gloves. Then Zora snapped on a second set of gloves like she was going into battle. Because that's what the OR was to her. A battlefield. A place where she was the general focused on winning each war.

Zora looked at the monitor. The BP was still dropping. Dr. Latam confirmed that the patient had been given an antibiotic.

Jane Doe had already been prepped, so Zora made a vertical cut down the length of her abdomen. Blood splattered as she cut through the peritoneum and inserted the retractors. She worked quickly, packing laparotomy pads into all four quadrants of the abdomen to soak up the excess blood, while Dr. Graham inserted a suction catheter, which gurgled bright red blood into a glass reservoir.

Zora looked up. "How's the rhythm?"

"Sinus tach. Rate is up to one-forty," Dr. Latam responded.

Her hands searched quickly in the upper left quadrant for the bleeder. She found it—it was the left renal artery. Its edges were jagged as if cut off in a hurry, and it had not been tied off properly. It seemed the person who removed the kidney knew just enough about anatomy to be dangerous. It was leaking blood slowly but surely into the abdomen, spreading blood into all four quadrants.

"Systolic at seventy!" the anesthesiologist called out.

Zora clamped the bleeder down and tied it off properly, while Dr. Graham removed the laparotomy pads and inserted fresh ones. They quickly turned red. Christina now held the suction catheter in place.

"She is still bleeding," Graham said.

"Systolic at fifty!" the anesthesiologist called out. The erratic beep from the monitor filled the air.

Zora's face remained still like granite. There was still another errant bleeder, and she needed to find it fast. Her hands moved with military precision to check the liver and the spleen as Dr. Graham kept replacing the laparotomy pads. She didn't bother with the aorta; if it was the culprit, the patient would have been a goner by now. No bleeding from the liver. Check. Zora moved to the spleen. She first divided the avascular ligaments to mobilize the spleen into the operating field, and then applied an atraumatic clamp to the splenic pedicle to secure the splenic artery and vein. She inspected the spleen and noted a major laceration on the side.

Whoever had removed the kidney seemed to have been careless and injured the spleen. A hack job.

"Systolic is now at sixty."

Zora forged on. Her work was not done. "Three-oh prolene," she barked.

Christina handed it to her. Zora used horizontal mattress sutures and pledgets to quickly stitch the lacerated edges together. She then applied fibrin glue to the raw edges. The bleeding was now barely visible.

"BP is back at ninety-five over fifty."

The steady beep of the monitor now reigned. The room seemed to heave a sigh as normalcy returned, as if it knew the critical part of the work had been completed.

Dr. Latam and the other OR nurses refused to say another word to her throughout the rest of the surgery, and by the time Zora was closing up the patient, the anesthesiologist was gone. The OR nurses disappeared shortly thereafter till only Christina remained.

This time Zora followed the nurse as she wheeled Jane Doe from the recovery room into the SICU. Once Jane Doe was all set up and hooked to the monitor in her cubicle, Zora straightened the sheets to cover her torso, rechecked her IV lines, and fiddled with her chart.

"We'll take care of her."

Zora turned to see the SICU nurse-on-duty assigned to Jane Doe standing by her side. "You don't have to worry." The nurse smiled at her. "We've got this." Zora looked at her name tag. It said Keller.

"I know what you are worried about." Zora's lip turned up at the familiar voice. Christina's head bobbed into view. "I can also check her every hour if you like," she said.

"Would you?"

"Sure. Anything for my bestie." Christina swung her arm over Zora's shoulders. "Now, go rest. You look like death warmed over."

Zora wanted to stay. Jane Doe might disappear like John Doe. But she trusted Christina. And she really needed to sleep.

She covered her mouth as a yawn escaped from her.

"See, I was right. Now get out of here." Christina placed her hands on Zora's shoulders and pushed her toward the door.

Zora took a last look at the patient before leaving.

And prayed that Jane Doe would still be there when she came back.

11

D rake thought about last night as he waited for the minutes to count down before his call with his business partner. He hadn't been surprised at the cool reception he had received at the H Club. Most folks didn't know how to deal with him, and he was sure the rumors were everywhere about what had happened with Anna Hammond. Some called out a greeting; others pretended not to have seen him.

Drake's jaw muscle tightened. They were all pretenders. Some of them had done worse. He'd only been unfortunate in that his situation had come to light. But no one had been bold enough to say anything to his face. They probably guessed he was still unforgiving of anyone who crossed him. And they were right.

He'd been seated in one of the private alcoves, a step down from a private room. It had been a slight, but he'd pretended not to notice. It was a mistake that in the future they would have no choice but to correct. All they needed was a reminder of how cruel he could be.

One of the hostesses had made a joke about his sexual prowess. The comment had made other guests at the H Club look away or cough to clear their throats. A few had hidden their smiles. Drake had waved off the comment, a thin smile plastered on his face. But that was probably the last joke the girl made. Her body was at the bottom of the river, her sexual parts slashed to bits. Her disappearance from the club would send a clear message—Drake was not someone to mess with.

He looked at his watch. It was time. As if on cue, a special grey burner phone that he had secured for the business started ringing. Drake picked up the phone from the top of his desk and pressed the answer button. The caller on the other end went straight to the point. "I see our plan is going very well," he said, his voice distorted on purpose. Drake hated that he couldn't identify who his business partner was, but the money was too good, so he ignored the minor inconvenience.

"I've heard there has been no problem," Drake responded.

"Of course not. Your latest payment has been deposited into your account as usual. We've also gotten more buyers who are interested, so I held back some of your funds like we agreed. This will allow us to expand even more."

"Are you sure they are clean? Secrecy is of the utmost importance here."

"Not a problem. These guys are not saints. We have enough on them to keep them quiet if they ever think about betraying us."

"I hope so."

"You don't need to concern yourself with them. You continue to play your part, and I'll take care of mine."

"Anything else?"

"I can see our friend Zora is getting flustered." The guy on the other line chuckled. "She's interesting to watch."

For some reason, his tone annoyed Drake. He had no business being fascinated with Zora. Zora belonged to Drake and him alone. And he never shared his women. He'd only brought Zora into his plan because he needed to punish her. "Let's stick to the plan, shall we?" he said.

A tinge of anger laced his partner's voice. "I can do whatever I want with her. Don't ever tell me what to do."

An uncomfortable silence stretched between them. Drake hadn't been sure in the beginning, but he'd come to suspect that he was dealing with a lunatic—someone who sometimes couldn't be reasoned with. *I can't believe I have to be the one to back down.* But the money from the business had become too important—he needed a lot of cashflow in the near future, and this business would provide it. It was unfortunate that this madman was in the driver's seat.

"Just take it easy with her," Drake finally said.

His partner laughed, his voice grating on Drake's nerves. Then he ended the call.

Drake replaced the phone in his desk drawer and scoffed. The madman had no idea that his business arrangement with Drake would end very soon. Drake just needed to hold on a little longer and then everything would be over. He would ask Monkey to find out all he could about the guy. He needed some evidence over the guy's head to be able to walk away whenever he wanted. And now he had to keep a closer eye on Zora. His instincts told him that his business partner was up to no good. He didn't care if Zora got hurt or not, but he had to be the only one with the power to punish her.

He pulled out the black burner phone and called Monkey. He didn't answer so Drake disconnected the call. He then pressed a hidden button under the surface of his desk and leaned back in his swivel chair.

The door to his office opened, and Tiny stepped in, looking like he had just showered in sweat.

Drake crinkled his nose in disgust. Seeing Tiny these days irritated him, but he kept him around because he was still useful. "I need you to keep a closer eye on Zora," he barked. "I want a thorough update."

"Any specific reason?"

"I pay you to obey not to ask questions!"

Tiny kept silent.

"It's time to set up the meeting with my father." Drake continued.

Tiny nodded in assent.

Drake waved him away. "You can go." Tiny left the room.

Drake ran his hands through his hair. This was what he got for working with someone for too long. One of these days he would get rid of Tiny.

In the meantime, he'd get Monkey to find him the information he needed and also watch Zora.

Because contrary to what the madman thought, Drake had the final say over her.

The man's phone buzzed in his pocket. He ignored it, but it kept ringing. "Excuse me," he said to his colleagues. He strode out of the room and walked down the hallway to the small conference room on the left. The white walled room with a small oval table, black swivel chairs, and a projector from the ceiling was empty. He entered and locked the door behind him, and then pressed the green button on the phone. "You know better than to call me here," he said.

"I'm sorry, boss," Erik said. "It's Monkey. You said for him to call immediately if he had important information."

"Yes?"

"Mr. Pierce asked him to watch over Dr. Smyth."

The man rapped his fingers on the conference table. That slime ball. *So he thinks Zora is his,* he thought. The man chuckled.

"What would you like him to do, boss?"

"Tell Monkey to share with him whatever he wants to know about Zora. Anything else?"

"Well …"

"Spit it out already."

"Mr. Pierce also wanted him to find out whatever he could about you."

The man cursed under his breath. So Pierce was trying to get a one up on him. Which only meant one thing—Pierce wanted to end the arrangement. Unfortunately for Pierce, this was his one no-no in this business. Anybody who'd tried to find out who he was had ended up in a watery grave. Pierce had crossed the line.

"What should he do, boss?"

Too bad that this was an arrangement that Pierce would never be able to walk away from. He'd chosen him for that reason. No one would miss the guy when he disappeared. Besides, something irked him about the pompous rapist. "Tell him to take care of Pierce. Nice and clean."

"Yes, boss."

"Hold on. You know what? Let him string him

along for a few days. I'll let him know when to go ahead and take care of him."

"I'll tell him, boss."

"And don't call me here again."

"Sorry, boss."

The man ended the call and checked his watch. He'd been gone for too long. He was sure his colleagues were looking for him.

He straightened his coat. Time to get back to work.

He opened the door to the conference room and walked away.

Christina woke up with a start. She'd fallen asleep on the chair she was sitting on at the SICU nursing station. Instead of coming and going, she'd chosen to remain and watch over the patient, and the SICU nurses had been kind enough to allow her to stay.

She wasn't supposed to have been on-call. It had been one of those days where her schedule couldn't be matched with Zora's no matter how much she tried. But the heavens must have been watching, because she'd gotten a call from a friend and colleague who was on the schedule today. She had to rush home to attend to her young child after the babysitter called her about an emergency. Could Christina stand-in for her?

No one else was available to come in at such short

notice, and the shift was extra busy today. Her director had already okayed it since Christina had significant OR experience at Lexinbridge Regional. So Christina had jumped at the chance. She figured being on duty at the same time as Zora even if not in the ER would still allow her to watch over her.

And then it turned out Zora had a Jane Doe to operate on. The missing name alerted Christina that this case might be similar to the one Zora had talked about. Perfect. Christina kept her eyes open as she prepped for the surgery. She'd never seen the anesthesiologist before, which was strange. Most anesthesiologists-on-call would typically come to the ER to see patients that were going up for emergency surgery, and yet this was the first time she'd met him. She couldn't be certain about the other scrub nurses, since she didn't work in the OR regularly.

By the time Jane Doe's surgery was over, her colleague had returned. Her aunt had arrived to look after the child, so Christina had been let off the hook. She hadn't been ready to go home yet. It had been an easy decision to offer to look after Jane Doe on Zora's behalf.

But a noise had woken her up. Christina listened and heard the sound again—the squeaky sound reminiscent of bed frame caster wheels that needed addi-

tional lubrication. And it came from the direction of
Jane Doe's cubicle. She looked at her watch. It was two
a.m. She looked around but couldn't see Nurse Keller.
Was she the one in there making adjustments to Jane
Doe's bed? It was time to find out.

Christina walked over to the cubicle and tapped her
badge against the reader on the wall. It slid open and
she stepped in. There was no one else in the room, and
Jane Doe was still lying there, the rise and fall of her
chest a reminder that all was as it should be. Yet she was
sure she had heard the sound coming from the room.

After looking around once more, Christina left the
room and looked down the hallway. She noticed a
gurney a few feet away, and she walked over to it. She
pushed the gurney, and it made a squeaky sound. *So
this is where the noise was coming from,* she thought. But
why was it in the hallway? She hung around for a few
minutes to see if anyone would claim it. No one did.

She felt a pressure in her lower abdomen. *Not now.,*
she thought. But the increasing strain told her she
couldn't put it off. And it would only take a few
minutes. She left the SICU, passed the waiting area,
and walked to the bathrooms located outside the area.
Once she was done, Christina headed back to the
SICU. On her way in, she noticed two burly men
wearing scrubs, surgical caps, and masks wheeling a

patient on a gurney toward the back elevators used for transporting patients to other areas of the hospital. She heard the squeaky sound again. *It's the gurney,* she thought. But what gave the men away were their shoes. They wore regular leather shoes, something that health professionals who worked in the SICU would never wear. And they were uncovered.

Her heart rammed against the wall of her chest. Something was wrong with this picture. Could it be Jane Doe on the gurney? Christina hurried into the SICU and checked her cubicle. Jane Doe was gone, her bed empty. She turned to see Nurse Keller working at one of the computer terminals at the central nursing station.

"Where is Jane Doe?" Christina asked.

"She was just transported to radiology for an MRI," Nurse Keller responded.

"By two guys?"

"Yes." So it was as she thought.

"But I don't recall Dr. Smyth putting in an order for one."

"I wondered too, but the order is in the system. Come and see."

Christina hastened around the central station, and sure enough the order was there signed off by Zora Smyth. Yet something smelled fishy about the whole thing. She thanked the nurse and ran to the elevators. She looked up and noted the elevator they had entered had stopped at parking level one instead of the base-ment level where the MRI center was located.

Bingo. Her instincts were right. Christina jabbed the buttons for the second elevator and jumped in when the doors slid open. She rode it down to parking level one, all the while praying that she could still catch up to them. She pulled out her phone and called Zora's number, but it went to voicemail. "Zora, pick up your phone!" she muttered.

The elevators opened on the parking floor, and Christina ran out. She looked left and right, but she didn't see anyone. The garage seemed silent as a grave. She made to turn back to the elevator when she spied what looked like the open door of an ambulance swinging close. Christina sprinted in that direction and saw one of the men walking toward the passenger side of the ambulance.

"Hey!" Christina shouted.

The man turned and looked at her.

The next thing Christina knew, a muscled arm grabbed her from behind, and another covered her mouth. She had forgotten about the second guy. Christina struggled with all her might to free herself. But from the way she was held, these were arms that knew what they were doing. She was ready to throw a backward leg kick at her assailant's groin when she felt the cold metal of the assailant's gun pressed against her temple. A black town car appeared, and the arms holding her shoved her toward it.

Christina's mind raced as she landed in the back seat of the car, and the assailant followed her in. It had been foolhardy to tackle this on her own, and now nobody knew she'd been taken.

As her eyes darted around to see if there was some weapon she could use, something hit her at the back of her neck.

Her world went black.

"Help me!" Zora's sister's hand reached out to her. A black windy force grabbed her sister's feet and pulled her away. A primal scream erupted from her as she flailed her hands.

Zora scrambled to move, but her legs were held down. She stretched out her hands to reach for her sister, but they came back empty.

"Help me!" her sister moaned.

Zora's heart pounded, and she pulled at her legs to release them. But she couldn't move no matter how much she tried.

Then her sister's hands slowed their dance as if drained of life. The black wind dragged her, flinging her like a ragged doll.

Zora's heart leapt, threatening to erupt. She struggled and jerked against what held her feet.

"Help me!" her sister whispered. "Help me ..." she continued, her voice now hoarse and monotonous. Then her face morphed into Jane Doe.

Zora jerked awake on the bed. Her heart pounded in her chest, and rivulets of sweat ran down her face. A feeling of foreboding enveloped her. She only dreamt about her sister when something bad was happening in her life.

It took Zora a minute to orient herself. She looked around as she took deep breaths. She was in the call room, and light streamed in between the curtains. She must have fallen asleep after leaving Jane Doe.

Jane Doe. Zora scrambled from the bed, put on her slip-on shoes, and raced to the SICU. She reached Jane Doe's cubicle and rushed in. The bed was empty.

Zora's heart picked up its pace. She hurried back to the SICU central station and met a different nurse sorting through some notes.

"Do you know where Jane Doe is?" Zora asked her.

"Jane Doe? Give me one second." The nurse typed into the computer in front of her. Then she lifted her eyes at Zora. "There is no Jane Doe here."

Zora's chest tightened. This couldn't be happening again.

"She was the patient in the cubicle on the far right." Zora pointed to the cubicle.

The nurse shook her head. "No patient was handed over from that cubicle," she insisted.

What the name again? That's right, Keller, she thought. "What about Nurse Keller that was on duty last night?"

"She's gone. Her shift is over."

"Can you reach her? It's important. Please."

"Let me call her cellphone number." The nurse pulled out a phone from her pocket, punched a few buttons on it, held it against her ear, but then shook her head.

Zora swallowed hard and sagged against the counter. *Not again.* Nurse Keller and Christina had promised her they'd look after Jane Doe. Christina.

"What about Christina?" she asked the nurse.

"Christina who?" The nurse gave her a blank stare. "I just started here two weeks ago, and I don't know her."

Zora gripped the edge of the counter.

She needed to find Christina. Now.

15

Zora pulled out her phone to call Christina and saw the missed calls. They were from a few hours ago. Her heart quickened. Maybe it was about Jane Doe. She called Christina's number, but the call went straight to voicemail. Strange.

Though Christina seemed to have worked an OR call, Zora expected her to be back either at the ER or at home by now. So she called the ER next. The nurse-on-duty stated that Christina had probably left for the day since she wasn't working the morning shift, but she hadn't seen her when she left. It was possible she was still in the hospital.

Making up her mind to go look for Christina herself, Zora hurried down the hallway that led to the

ER. She met Stewart on her way in. He was about to leave, his hands in the pockets of his medical coat.

"Dr. Smyth, is everything okay? You don't look too good."

"I'm looking for Nurse Christina. Have you seen her?"

"Your roommate, right?" At Zora's widened eyes, "It's no secret. Everyone knows. I saw her last night when I came by to pick up something from the hospital. Do you want me to help you look for her?"

"Could you?"

"Sure. Why don't you look for her on this side of the ER?" He gestured to the right. "I'll take the other side."

"Thank you." Zora strode down the right side and checked each cubicle. Some cubicles were empty, but most were filled with patients that had been admitted overnight. Christina was not in any of them. She checked the last cubicle and then turned back to the central station. She spoke with the nurses. No one had seen Christina that morning. She had them look up Jane Doe's records. Nothing. And the nurses had never heard of a Dr. Latam—a different anesthesiologist had been on-call. Zora's hand tugged her pendant. It was happening all over again. She checked for her operative reports. They were missing too. But this time Zora was ready; she had printed a copy of her operative report after she had submitted it into the system. They were in her locker in the call room.

Stewart ran up to meet her. "Did you find her?" he asked. Zora shook her head. "She wasn't in any of the cubicles. I even asked one of the other nurses to check their break room and the bathroom. She wasn't there. Are you sure she hasn't gone home?"

"She might have. Thanks for helping out. Don't let me keep you."

Stewart smiled at her. "No worries. Glad I could help. I'll see you later." He walked out of the ER.

Zora walked back into the hallway. Where was Christina? She tried her number again. "Pick up, Christina, pick up," she muttered to herself. It went to voicemail. This was not good. Now, two people were missing—Jane Doe and Christina. Had something bad happened to Christina? Zora fiddled with her pendant and prayed that wasn't the case. Maybe there was no need to worry yet. She could just be at home sleeping off the call and had switched off her phone. Yes, that was it. There was no way Christina would have disappeared.

So where was Jane Doe? Zora had no idea where to

look next. This was the second missing patient. She could not turn a blind eye to it anymore. Something was going on, and it was time to bring it to the attention of the hospital leadership.

But she still needed more evidence; the operative reports were not enough. There were three other people who had been involved in Jane Doe's case—Dr. Graham, Nurse Keller, and the attending who had been on-call. She hadn't been able to reach Nurse Keller, which left two people in the hospital she still needed to talk to. There was no way one of them couldn't serve as a witness. Her thoughts were preoccupied as she walked down the hallway, and by the time she looked up, she had ended up in front of Dr. Edwards' office. She might as well go in and get his advice.

Zora knocked on his door and stepped in to see Dr. Edwards staring at a set of CT scan films clipped to the screen on the wall of his office.

"Zora, what do you think?" Dr. Edwards gestured at the films. He was distinguished-looking with a strong angular jaw, square chin, and greyed temples.

Zora stepped closer to the screen to examine the films. "Is this for a new patient?"

"No, a patient I've seen a few times in my clinic."

Zora's eyes moved slowly from one film to the next. "Isn't this pseudomyxoma peritonei?" she asked. She could see indications of voluminous mucinous ascites—the scalloped indentation of the liver and spleen, and the rim-like calcifications with some septation. Her fingers traced the surface of the film.

"But it could also be peritoneal mucinous carcinomatosis," Dr. Edwards replied.

"True. But see"—Zora pointed to an area on the film—"there are no tumor nodules in the peritoneum and there is no invasion of the small bowel. Those are signature effects of peritoneal mucinous carcinomatosis."

Dr. Edwards nodded, his eyes twinkling. "So what would you do for this patient?"

Zora turned to face Dr. Edwards. "It depends on the condition of the patient. My first preference would be a modified cytoreductive surgery, in which you would first debulk the mucinous buildup, then remove the affected tissues, and finally insert the chemotherapy drugs. Patients not qualified for surgery would receive chemotherapy only, though it may not cure the disease."

Dr. Edwards nodded, his face wrinkling into a smile. "Good work, Zora."

"This is such a rare case. I've never been in a surgery for it."

Dr. Edwards laughed. "Okay, okay. I'll pen you down as a first assist. Happy now?"

"Yes!" Then Zora's face morphed into a frown. "I actually came to see you about something else."

Zora told him about Jane Doe and how she had disappeared.

"This is serious." Dr. Edwards folded his arms over his chest and leaned against his desk.

"I know. I think it's time I mentioned it to Dr. Anderson."

"Do you have enough evidence?"

"Well, I have a copy of my operative report."

"That's a good start, but I'm not sure it is enough. Getting evidence is what is most important. Remember you need to tread carefully with him. There is no need to rock the boat unnecessarily, I say."

"But this is about a patient's life!" Zora ran her hands through her hair as she removed the hair tie. "I'm sorry. It's just that the patient has sepsis and needs close monitoring. She could die otherwise."

Dr. Edwards' eyes scanned her face through his oval glasses. "Have you spoken to Dr. Graham about it? You said he was the first assist for the surgery."

"Not yet. I plan to ask him before the round, though I'm not very optimistic about what he'll say."

"Okay, speak to him. And then try and get any other evidence you can."

Zora glanced at her watch. "Speaking of rounds, I need to head out now in order to make it. I'll talk to you later."

Zora felt Dr. Edwards' eyes on her as she left his office. But she had made up her mind. It didn't matter at this point what the department chair thought about her. A patient disappearing from the hospital was a big deal and needed to be reported.

And no one could tell her otherwise.

Zora met Graham outside the entrance to the acute care general surgical unit on her way to the round. He was speaking in Russian to someone on the phone. Zora had had a roommate from Russia in college, so she recognized the language. Zora shook her head. Unbelievable! Who would have thought that Graham could speak Russian so fluently? Clearly, she didn't know enough about him after all the years they had worked together. But that wasn't why she was here waiting for him. Time to refocus.

She waited for his call to finish and then pulled him to the side before he could enter the surgical unit.

"Zora, what is this about?" Graham brushed off Zora's hand from his arm like he was swatting a fly and straightened the sleeves of his long white medical coat.

"Do you remember the patient we operated on last night?"

The corners of his lips curled downward. "What patient are you talking about? I wasn't in the hospital last night."

If it was possible for Zora's jaw to drop open to the floor from where she stood, it would have. "What are you talking about? You mean you don't remember Jane Doe?"

"Zora, this must be some kind of joke. And it's not funny." Dr. Graham let out a deep sigh. "Look, the round is going to start in the next five minutes, and I can't stand here listening to this gibberish." He tugged at his mustache. "Let's be frank here, Zora. I've been hearing odd things about you. And I'm sure I'm not the only one."

Zora stilled. "What sort of odd things?"

A sardonic smile filled his face. "You performing surgery on patients that do not exist and asking the medical staff strange questions about patients. Even the junior residents have been whispering behind your back. Don't you think you need some sort of help? You are giving chief residents a bad name." He tucked his hands into the pockets of his medical coat. "Go see a therapist before it's too late." He shook his head and walked off into the unit.

Zora tensed, and her nostrils flared. She had never really cared for Graham. Now, she thoroughly disliked him. She should have known nothing good could come from talking to him.

She took a couple of deep breaths. She had a job to do first, and her patients were waiting.

But she would not give up.

She still had one more person to ask.

Zora's mind wandered as the round went on. Luckily, there were other patients apart from hers that the group could focus on. And when she was called upon, she knew enough about her patients to present on autopilot.

As soon as the round ended, Zora hurried to the attending who had been on-call last night. He was speaking with some interns, so Zora waited till he finished.

"Dr. Smyth, how can I help you?" The attending was a no-nonsense guy who didn't like to mince words.

Zora needed a break in the case. And this was most

likely it. If it didn't work out, then maybe she needed to start considering that something was really wrong with her like they said.

She took a deep breath. *Here goes nothing.* "I was wondering if you remembered my call about a patient last night."

16

Christina opened her eyes to see she was in what looked like a warehouse. It would have been dark except for the light streaming in from one window that was partly open on her left. She could make out some large drums with dark colored stains all over them piled in a corner ahead of her. She tried to rub her eyes and then realized that her hands were immobile. She looked down to see that they were tied behind her back with a thick rope that also looped around a beam. And her legs were held together with a zip tie that cut into her skin. Christina bit her lower lip to stop herself from crying out in pain.

She heard the footsteps that echoed in the room before she saw him. He was bulky with a meaty head heralded by a forehead that looked as flat as a saucepan.

He towered over her, and Christina resisted the urge to shrink back.

She couldn't let the fear paralyze her. Even though she didn't know who these guys were, it was clear they were up to no good and could easily get rid of her if they so chose. But what was more important was that no one knew she was missing. And it might be too late for her by the time Zora pieced it together. She had to send her a message. An idea came to her.

"I taped the surgery," she blurted out.

The bulky man cast an intense gaze on her. Christina wasn't sure if he believed her.

"I had a camera in the girl's surgery, and I recorded the whole thing," she insisted.

The man remained silent. And then he pulled a phone from his pocket and made a call. Christina figured it was his boss on the other end of the line, someone who understood Russian.

Then he placed a hand over the phone. "Where is it?" the man bellowed at her.

"In my apartment. But you won't be able to find it unless I show you. It's hidden somewhere very secret."

The man spoke again to the person on the other line.

Christina waited with bated breath. *God, I need*

your help, she prayed. If they didn't believe her, she wasn't sure how long they would keep her alive.

The bulky man ended the call and motioned to someone behind her who she hadn't been aware was there.

Christina's pulse ratcheted up. Maybe they had decided to just kill her and get it over with. Someone touched her back. Christina jumped, but the ropes held fast. She felt the hands tugging at the ropes, and then they fell away.

The new man grabbed her hands before she could move them, bound them with a cable tie, and then cut the tie at her feet. "All done, Thunder," he said to the first man in a Russian accent.

"Get up," Thunder barked.

Christina struggled to her feet and glanced at the nameless man behind her. He could practically be Thunder's twin.

Then a hood fell over her head, and Christina lost all sense of direction.

"Move," Thunder said. Christina shuffled forward as Twinny pushed her from behind.

She had no idea where they were going, but she hoped that meant she still had a chance to live.

Christina was bundled into a car, and they drove around for a while before the car stopped. The hood was pulled from her head, and that was when Christina realized they were right in front of Zora's apartment.

She let out a sigh of relief. The boss on the other line must have chosen to go along with her story. She still had a chance to escape.

Twinny opened the car door and then pulled her from the backseat. Christina looked around. The street was quiet, and no one was out and about. She couldn't cry for help. It was just her luck that there were no neighbors loitering on the sidewalk.

Twinny nudged her toward the steps that led to her apartment. Christina climbed the steps, her mind racing to see if there were any escape options. By now, Thunder had gotten out of the car and climbed the front stairs to open the main building entrance door. Christina noticed he held her keys in his gloved hands. *He must have taken them from my pocket when I was unconscious,* she thought.

Twinny pushed her into the building, and Christina made it to her floor sandwiched between them. Thunder used her keys again to unlock the door, while Twinny pushed her inside and shut the door behind them. The smell of the pecan pie she had made in the morning still hung in the air, and her stomach rumbled. Which reminded her she hadn't eaten anything since last night.

"Bring it." Thunder barked.

Christina shrugged her shoulders and pivoted to raise her tied hands at him.

"Show us."

Christina's shoulders fell. So they had no plans to untie her hands. It was just little her against mighty them. What did they think she could do? Her mind raced for other alternatives as she slowed her steps to her room. She needed to buy time. Maybe time for Zora to come home or for one of the neighbors to come outside. She only had a chance to escape if there was someone else around beside these goons.

Once she got to the front of her door, she waited till Thunder opened it. Christina stepped in and ignored the fact that these goons had just invaded her private haven. Apart from Zora, she'd never allowed anyone into her little slice of heaven. Zora had given her free hand to decorate the room like she wanted, and Christina had let her fantasy run wild. Literally. It was a safari-inspired room with its large African sunset photograph-turned-wallpaper on one wall, an adjoining faux gator skin back wall behind the headboard, a cheetah spotted rug on the floor and wooden engraved chairs, paired with other modern pieces. Tribal printed pillows completed the safari-chic look. She clenched her teeth in a tight smile and headed for what had brought her here. The panic toy.

Zora had bought it for her as a gift a couple of years ago. The green toy with its red button made a maddening sound that Christina hated. But it had one thing in its favor. Christina could program a phone number into it. And once the panic button was pressed, it would flash a green light and send a "Help" text message to the owner of the phone number.

Christina had harassed Zora with text messages till she begged her to stop. It was a strange little toy, but Zora had seemed excited when she gave it to her, so Christina had kept it. She'd been cleaning her room last week and had found it tucked into a corner of her closet. She'd moved it to a box figuring that it might be useful someday. She'd had no idea it would be today.

Christina went on her knees and swung her tied hands under the queen-sized bed to hook and pull out the shoe box she'd stored the toy in. She used both hands to push the box cover off. She'd never been so glad to see the toy. She pressed the red button before they could stop her.

There was no green light. Christina jabbed it again and again as she felt hands pull her roughly away from the box. There was no response. And then it dawned on her. The battery must have run out. *Christina, how could you be so stupid?* she thought.

"Where's the tape?" Thunder asked.

Christina ignored them and continued jabbing the toy she held in her hands, hoping that it would come alive even for one second. A hand smacked her across the cheek and pulled away the toy.

She didn't feel the sting. It was like it was happening to someone else. *I've failed. Why didn't I check the battery when I first found it?* she thought.

Christina felt a hard object strike her temple, and a flash of pain swept through her head. The small toy in Thunder's meaty hands was the last thing she saw before she passed out.

17

"Of course I remember the patient," the attending said to Zora. "You're talking about Jane Doe, right?"

It was like the heavens had opened and the angels were singing. Zora's eyes welled up with tears. She didn't know whether to cry or laugh. She gripped his arm. "Thank you, thank you, thank you."

He looked pointedly at his arm, and she realized what she had done. She let go and backed away a little. The attending cleared his throat. "I came in this morning to look her up, but I didn't find her in the system. I meant to ask you about her after the round," he said. "Has she been discharged?"

"No, that's the thing. I can't find her in the SICU, and all her medical records are gone."

"That's strange. I called the SICU last night to ask about her, and even made some notes in her medical record. I like to keep copies of my notes, so I have one in my car. "

Zora's heart leaped with joy. More evidence. Her day suddenly looked brighter. "Do you think I could make a copy of it? I'm planning to see Dr. Anderson about her."

"I can show them to you later. I still have patients on this floor I need to see. I could always provide a copy if there ends up being an investigation. But in the meantime let me know how your discussion with Dr. Anderson goes."

"Thanks again."

"No problem." The attending turned back and headed to the bedside of one of the patients in the unit.

Zora smiled and walked away. The attending had no idea what he had just done. He had saved her life. Even though Zora had been sure the surgeries took place, she'd started wondering if she was paranoid, or even worse, crazy. With everyone telling her otherwise, it had been a little overwhelming. One person believed her, and if she could get home soon and talk with Christina, that would make two people.

But for now, she still had to see her remaining patients.

And then she would go talk with Dr. Anderson.

18

"D r. Smyth, how can I help you?" Dr. Anderson asked. Zora sat facing him in the same chair she had sat in the last time she was here. The only difference was that the office was more disorganized today. Zora wondered how he was able to find anything he needed. "Julie said you had something urgent to discuss."

Zora twiddled her thumbs in her lap. It wasn't so easy to just spill it out now that she was here.

She took a deep breath and exhaled. There was no point in beating about the bush. "Two patients have gone missing in the past few days."

Dr. Anderson leaned forward, and his brow furrowed. "Missing? What do you mean?"

Zora told him about the patients that had appeared

with missing kidneys, how they and their records had vanished, how one of the attendings could corroborate her story, and how she was trying to touch base with another witness. Zora made no mention of Graham's role in the surgery, since it might offend the department chair and turn him against whatever she had to say. Zora saw his face change from skepticism to concern and worry.

"Why didn't you come to me when the first patient went missing?" he said.

"It was only my word against everyone else, and I didn't have the evidence to back it up."

Dr. Anderson ran a jerky hand through his hair. "This is a big deal. And there are major repercussions if what you've said is true. You should have come to me immediately." Dr. Anderson pressed his intercom. "Julie, I need you to get Ms. James and Mr. Sanders to my office immediately." Zora recognized the names as the Chief Medical Information Officer and the Privacy and Security Officer respectively. "Tell them that it's urgent. Thank you." He removed his finger from the intercom. "Dr. Smyth, I'm glad you've told me. I'll take it from here. Why don't you head back to work? I'll let you know if we need anything else from you."

Zora nodded and got up. She felt a bit lighter—it was like a weight had been lifted off her shoulders, though she still had to make sure that Christina was okay. Dr. Edwards had been wrong about Dr. Anderson. It was obvious that patients were still his number one priority despite all the intradepartmental squabbles.

She left his office and headed out.

It was time to head home and hopefully track Christina down.

19

But when Zora got home in the late afternoon and looked around the living room, Christina was nowhere to be seen. In fact, it seemed she had not made it home. Christina had a habit of dropping her work shoes—the ones she wore once she got off work—by the door, and they were not yet there. Even if she had somewhere else to be, she'd typically come home first to wash off the stink from the hospital. Unless it was an impromptu visit or appointment, and she had decided to go straight there instead of coming home first.

She tried Christina's number again. Her phone was now switched off. Which probably meant that Christina had seen her missed calls before turning off her phone. But why hadn't she called Zora back?

Hmmm. Maybe she was somewhere where she couldn't take calls. Still, Zora would give Christina a good talking to the next time she saw her for making her worry for nothing.

Zora let out an exhale and felt her shoulders relax. Christina would most likely be home by tonight. She was a homebody who never liked to spend the night anywhere else—she called her bed "the comfort palace." Zora had teased her many times about it.

Zora dipped into the couch and stretched out her limbs, placing her phone on the couch beside her. She was bone tired. Her stomach growled as she stifled a yawn. Definitely hungry as well, but that was of lower priority. She closed her eyes. Only a few minutes of rest would do.

Zora opened her eyes to the ringing of her phone. The room had grown dark, and the mint green and silver polka dot curtains kept the setting sun away. She stretched out her hand to look for her phone and fell off the couch. *Ouch.* Zora rubbed her bottom where it had hit the floor as she listened for where the Christmas ringtone was coming from. She crawled forward in the direction of the sound till she found it wedged where the side table met the couch. She picked it up and swiped the green button.

"This is Zora Smyth."

"Hello, Dr. Smyth. This is Nurse May from the OR. We've been trying to reach Christina, but her phone is switched off. Could you connect her for us?"

"Hold on." Zora walked toward Christina's room. She should be home by now. "Christina!" There was no response. She reached her room and opened the door.

"Oh my Lord!" Zora said as she staggered back.

The room looked like a tornado had blown through. Christina's bed was completely torn apart and in total disarray. Clothes spilled from her wardrobe and trailed on the rug. The bedside lamp had been knocked down, and shards of the lampshade lay scattered on the floor. Her nursing books were strewn all over her desk with some pages ripped away. One of her engraved wooden chairs was upside down, the other flung to the side.

As Zora tried to comprehend what had happened, she noticed a sparkly item on the floor, and she bent to pick it up. It was Christina's pendant—a gold cross with a diamond embedded in the center—with its clasp broken. Christina always wore it. It had been a gift from her father who had died four years ago from prostate cancer. Zora had never seen her without it. Christina would never leave her pendant at home, unless ...

A shudder ran through Zora's body, and she backed away from the room. She lifted the phone with trembling hands to her ear and tried to keep her voice light. "Christina is not here at the moment. I'll let her know you called once I reach her."

Zora ended the call.

Zora hurried to her own room. Everything was in its place. She checked the spare room. Nothing was missing. She walked back to the living room and looked around. There was no evidence that anything had been moved.

Zora paced the living room. Christina was a neat freak, and she adored her special space. A safari trip to Africa had been her last holiday with her father before he passed away, and some of the pieces in her room were from that trip. There was no way she would have left her room in such disarray. There was only one other explanation: someone had been to their apartment.

Zora shuddered and her stomach churned. She should have noticed sooner. Something terrible must have happened to Christina—the ransacked room plus her disappearance didn't add up to anything normal. It was really unlike Christina to just vanish without noti-fying anyone. And she had never missed a shift before.

Zora couldn't shake the feeling away. Christina might be in danger. And she just happened to be the only other person who'd been in the OR with her and watched the Jane Doe surgery take place.

Zora unlocked her phone screen with a shaky hand to call Detective Dave McKesson. Dave had gone to high school with Zora and Christina. In fact, Zora had dated Dave for a short time. But when her sister was kidnapped, Zora had withdrawn from everyone, including Dave, and the relationship had fallen apart. Only Christina had been persistent and refused to leave her alone.

Zora had sometimes seen him at the annual high school reunion. She'd heard he was working out of state with the New York City Police Department. Christina had managed to remain in touch with him over the years and had mentioned last Christmas that Dave had transferred back to Lexinbridge and was now with the local PD. As Christina explained it, an exception had been made in his case, so he hadn't started as a rookie but as a detective.

Zora hoped he was still there. She hated dealing with the police. They had botched her sister's kidnapping case and had then tried to pin the blame on her family. And in recent years, they'd also tried to incriminate her in the formalin murders. Who knew what they would try to blame her for this time around? So it was best to talk to someone she was familiar with, if she had no choice but to deal with them, like in this case.

She called the police switchboard. "I would like to speak with Detective Dave McKesson."

"One moment please," a friendly voice replied and put her on hold.

A few seconds later, "This is Detective Dave McKesson." His voice sounded deep and rich, and made an unnamed sensation course through her.

Zora brushed the feeling away. This was not the time. Christina could be in danger. "This is Zora Smyth."

Zora heard his breath hitch over the line. "Hi, Zora. Long time," Dave managed to say.

"Yes it is. Dave …"

"Go ahead." His voice had now assumed a more business-like tone.

"It's Christina. I think she's missing." Zora choked back a cry.

"Where are you?" Dave asked, his voice an octave higher.

"I'm at home."

"I'll be right there." The phone clicked.

Zora wrapped her arms around herself. Uttering the words aloud had made them real. She started shivering.

She also realized she hadn't told Dave where she lived.

Zora was pacing the living room when she heard a banging on the door. She looked through the peephole, and the tension in her shoulders eased a little. She unclasped the lock and opened the door. Dave stood there, as handsome as ever. He had filled out from the scrawny kid she had dated into a lean machine with no extra fat. She wondered how he could look so good.

As he stepped into her apartment, Zora looked down at herself and grimaced. She hadn't even thought to change her clothes. She wore a wrinkled loose top that drowned her well-proportioned body, and pants that had seen better days.

"Nice place," Dave said, looking around.

Zora blurted out the first thing that came to mind.

"How did you know my address? I don't recall ever giving it to you."

"I asked the dispatcher to trace your address," he responded, fixing his piercing brown eyes on her.

Zora's face heated up. She was being a bumbling fool in front of the guy who had just made her skin tingle. Like he used to before. But this was not the right time to think about his effect on her.

Turning her eyes away, she motioned to the couch. "Please sit."

Dave perched on the edge of the couch, his long legs stretched out before him. "So what's this about Christina?"

Zora told him everything. About the patients with botched surgeries who had disappeared, their missing records, the ghost anesthesiologist and scrub team, and the attending who remembered her call. How she'd come home to find Christina's room trashed, and how Christina was only one of three people who could vouch that they'd been present at the surgery.

Dave wrote everything down. "Who are the others?"

"There's Dr. Ronald Graham. But he's denied the surgery happened. And then we have Nurse Keller, the SICU nurse that was assigned to Jane Doe. She was gone by the time I got to the SICU, and I haven't been able to reach her since."

Dave scribbled further in his notes.

"Let me show you Christina's room," she said.

Zora led him to the room and showed him the pendant. Dave chided her for not wearing gloves before picking it up.

Zora bristled. "Look, I wasn't thinking at that time that Christina might have been kidnapped."

"There's no need to get worked up. Always the spitfire."

Zora shot him a venomous look.

Dave grinned, but then turned serious again. "We typically advise that you wait twenty-four hours before filing a missing person's report. But with the way this is"—he swept his hands around the room—"we can consider it a case of kidnapping and have forensics come over."

Zora's throat grew thick. "Thank you. For taking me seriously." Seeing his questioning look, she said, "Everyone thinks I'm deluded and that I'm making things up."

Dave put his hand on her arm. "We'll do everything to find her," he stated in a firm tone.

A feeling of warmth flowed through her at his

touch. Zora choked up and couldn't speak. Instead, she nodded in agreement.

"Let me make a phone call," Dave said and walked a few feet away.

Zora looked around her apartment while Dave made the call. This place would never feel the same again. It had been a place of safety, refuge, and recharge. But it had been desecrated. The muscle in her jaw tightened just thinking about it.

Dave got off the phone and walked back to where Zora stood with her arms wrapped around herself. "Someone from forensics is on the way. I'll wait till they get here."

Zora's shoulders relaxed a bit. She had missed this. Dave had been a rock to lean on back in high school. She wondered why she'd never sought him out after she had somewhat come to terms with her sister's disappearance, though Zora had never lost hope that they'd find her. In fact, Marcus was constantly looking for new leads regarding the case, but nothing had panned out in recent times. Zora had accepted she needed to live her own life while still searching for her.

"Are you married?" she blurted out before she could stop herself. Heat rose on her face, and Zora wished the ground could open up and swallow her.

Dave chuckled. The dimples on his cheeks highlighted how gorgeous he was, and Zora felt the butter-flies in her stomach flutter in response. "No, I'm not," he said.

Zora had guessed that was the case—there was no ring on his finger—but it felt good to hear him say it. Then she remembered Christina.

She turned away and walked over to the kitchen to lean against the counter. What was she thinking? Christina was missing. Her heart lurched at the thought. Christina was all that mattered at the moment.

The silence between them grew awkward. "Can I get you anything? Water, coffee, soda?" she asked.

Dave looked at her, his eyes a tempting pool of chocolate. "I'm fine. Thanks for offering."

The silence increased until it became an elephant in the room.

Dave fiddled with his pen. "Zora, we'll do every-thing we can to find Christina."

Zora's fingers twisted her pendant back and forth. "I know you will," Zora responded. "I just wish she would walk in and say, 'Surprise!' but something tells me that's not going to happen."

"It's going to be—"

There was a knock at the door. Dave strode to the door and opened it. "Come in, Bill."

A short, potbellied guy that reminded Zora of a jolly Father Christmas walked in, flanked by a slim blonde with a camera around her neck.

Dave turned to Zora. "Bill is our forensic expert and the best in the area. Laura is our crime scene tech." Dave turned back to Bill. "Bill, this is Zora, a high school friend of mine. It appears her roommate might have been kidnapped."

Zora acknowledged them with a nod. "Thanks for coming over. The room in question is this way." Zora led them to the room and opened the door.

"Wow," said Laura.

Bill turned to Zora. "We'll take it from here."

"Why don't we get out of their way?" Dave said to Zora. "Is there a coffee shop nearby? Bill will give me a call once he's done."

"Give me a moment to change," Zora replied.

Dave looked her up and down. "You look fine to me. Beautiful as always."

Zora felt the heat on her cheeks. It had been a long time since any man really complimented her. Of course, she had fellow residents and patients who told her she looked great, but it was not the same. She'd been too busy to date in medical school and no less so in residency. "I'll b-be right b-b-back," she stammered and scurried to her room.

Five minutes later, she came out wearing a black and white T-shirt with "I'm No Rebel" written on it in red, and a pair of blue jeans matched with black boots. She had washed her face and her hair was piled up in a ponytail. "I'm ready to go. The coffee shop is a block away. We'll just walk there," she said.

Zora and Dave left the apartment and headed down the stairs. Her phone vibrated in her jean pocket. She pulled it out and looked at the screen. Brian Atkinson, her BFF and a surgical resident who was also in his fifth year, was calling her. They had grown close after Zora had tripped in the call room and poured coffee down his shirt in their first year of residency and had remained friends ever since.

Brian had graduated from Harvard Medical school before applying for a residency spot at Lexinbridge Regional. Rumors had it that he had included the hospital on his list during the matching process on a dare—he wasn't a small city kind of guy even though Lexinbridge Regional's general surgical residency program was one of the best in the country. The city must have changed him, because now he was planning to snag one of the fellowship spots at the hospital. He had been on vacation for the past one month and had likely gotten back earlier today.

Zora picked up the call. "Brian, welcome back. What's going on?"

"I'm so sorry, Zora."

Zora stopped walking, and her heart rate picked up. This was the first time Brian had ever said those words to her over their years of friendship. She noticed Dave had halted too.

"Brian, what's wrong?" Zora asked. Dave looked at her with eyebrows raised.

"I just heard the attendings discussing your suspension. What's going on?"

"Hold on. What suspension? There must be some kind of mistake."

"They didn't tell you? You should have gotten an email and a certified mail about it."

"Brian, I'll call you back." Zora disconnected the call and quickly pulled up her work email on her phone. Sure enough, there was an email marked "URGENT" from an ad hoc Disciplinary Committee. She quickly scanned the notice and collapsed against the wall.

Dave reached out to grab her. "What's going on, Zora?"

Zora shook her head in disbelief. "I've been suspended for a month. For misconduct pending further investigation. I don't understand. I've done nothing wrong …" Her voice trailed away as she stared out blankly. "Could it be …?"

She pulled herself to her feet abruptly. "I need to go. I'll call you later." She pushed off the wall and staggered down the stairs.

"Zora, wait!"

Zora picked up speed and raced down the remaining stairs and out into the street. The air was bitter cold, but she didn't feel a thing. She hailed the first cab she saw. "Lexinbridge Regional please," she said as she slid into the cab.

"You got it." The driver sped off. Within a few minutes, they'd arrived at the hospital entrance.

Zora jumped out and handed the driver a twenty. "Keep the change."

She sprinted through the hospital entrance and took the escalator to the fourth floor. Dr. Anderson's office was on the far right of the east wing. She marched down the hallway and stepped into the front office. His secretary, Julie, sat behind her desk, shuffling some papers. She looked up as Zora came in.

"I'm here to see Dr. Anderson," Zora said.

"He's leaving in about five minutes," Julie responded in an apologetic tone.

"It will only take a minute," Zora pleaded.

The secretary's eyes searched Zora's face for a moment. "Alright, go in. Good luck."

Zora turned away. The secretary had probably heard about her suspension. She wondered if others would look at her with pity as well.

She took a deep breath and knocked on the door to the inner office. She heard a faint reply come through the door.

Zora stepped into Dr. Anderson's office. He was standing behind his desk, taking a call.

"Yes, yes, I understand. Goodnight," he said to whoever was on the other end of the line. He finished the call and placed the phone on his desk.

"Dr. Smyth, I assume you are here about the disciplinary interview. Sit." He gestured to the visitors' seats as he sat down on his chair.

Zora pulled back one of the seats facing the desk and settled on it. She was beginning to think the chairs were unlucky with all the bad news and false promises she'd received while sitting on them. "I don't understand why I'm facing possible suspension. What have I done wrong? And which misconduct are we talking about?" she said in a tense voice.

"Well, you inappropriately took another patient's surgery slot without permission."

"That's old news, and I already got punished for it. I ended up with an extra three-day call and lost the opportunity to attend the GI conference," Zora pointed out.

"Unfortunately, both the doctor and the VIP patient complained. We have to take such complaints seriously, you understand."

"The VIP patient complained and I'm just hearing about it after a few days? We both know VIP patients air their grievances immediately. And besides, the VIP patient didn't experience any delays from their end. What's the real reason for the suspension?"

"Dr. Smyth, you've stepped on some really big toes up there with what you did." Dr. Anderson pointed upwards. "And management is not happy."

Zora shifted in her seat. "Which big toes? The VIP patient issue is not enough to warrant their attention. And suspension? That's like killing an ant with a sledgehammer. That's going to go in my record, which would affect my chances for a good fellowship spot. It will ruin my career!"

"Dr. Smyth, my hands are tied. There will be a disciplinary interview next week after which a recommendation will be forwarded to the Medical Executive Committee as to whether to keep you in the program or let you go."

"What?" Zora got up suddenly, knocking back her chair. "I can't believe this," she sputtered.

"I'm sorry, Dr. Smyth, there's nothing I can do." Dr. Anderson looked at his watch. "And I have to leave now. I have a meeting across town that I need to get to." He picked up his black jacket from the coat rack and donned it.

Zora staggered out of the inner office. The secretary was gone. It was just as well. Another look of pity might undo her. She exited the office into the hallway and leaned her back against the wall. "This cannot be happening to me," she whispered.

It was far worse than Zora had initially thought. *Something is wrong here,* she thought. A suspension seemed too much for just butting into someone's slot, especially since she had been in and out of the OR with more than enough time to prep for the next patient. No harm done, and the VIP patient wouldn't have been aware of any delay. Unless … no, it couldn't be. Was it because she had been asking about Jane Doe? But why would someone upstairs want to shut her up about it?

Zora shook her head. This was all too much. Two patients had disappeared, Christina was missing, and now this. "Aargh!"

A nurse passing by gave her a strange look and pushed her cart further away.

Zora fiddled with her pendant. She couldn't just stay here while her life was going up in smoke. She had to do something. Anything.

Zora turned her head and saw Dr. Anderson step out into the hallway with his black bag. She started toward him.

"Dr. Smyth, you are still here?"

"I have to ask. Is this whole case about the patients? The ones I reported missing?"

Dr. Anderson pushed his glasses up his nose. "Dr. Smyth, I don't know what you are talking about."

"What do you mean?" Zora cried. "I spoke to you earlier today about it."

"Dr. Smyth, I think everything has been too much for you lately. Time away from the hospital would do you good. I heard the rumors about you looking for missing patients, but I didn't believe it. This wouldn't look good for you in the disciplinary interview. I suggest you have a quick chat with a therapist."

"But—"

"Goodnight, Dr. Smyth." Dr. Anderson strode off down the hallway and disappeared from view.

Zora clenched her fists by her side. Unbelievable. In the blink of an eye, she had gone from being a witness to a culprit. So this was the stance Dr. Anderson was taking. Make her out to be unstable and then kick her from the program.

They—whoever the people upstairs were—had another thing coming if they thought she would just roll over and accept whatever they handed to her. This was an aggressive move, which meant something big was at stake here, something that had to stay hidden at all costs. And as a result, her life was zooming out of control. Her career had always been the one constant element in her life. To lose it now after all the years of sacrifice would be devastating.

She had to get to the bottom of this case or die trying.

22

Drake's eyes locked on his father's like magnets as they sat opposite each other in the restaurant. They were the only ones in the main area, but Drake could hear the distant clatter of plates being washed and cooking utensils hung up. The smell of roasted meat and fresh garlic bread saturated the air. It was his father's favorite restaurant, one that he and Drake's mother had eaten at once every month. Drake found the old-fashioned nature of the restaurant very stifling and had made up excuses to not attend during the years before he'd left home. He hadn't been back to the restaurant ever since.

But the place worked for today's meeting. He'd emptied the restaurant, something his father had never been able to accomplish—a demonstration that their roles had changed—since the owner was very fastidious about making sure his loyal customers who came in every day had access to the restaurant anytime they liked. But Drake had found the guy's pain point and made it go away, which earned him an empty restaurant whenever he wanted.

The meeting had been a long time coming. Drake had been bitter against his father since the day he cut him off from the company. He hadn't expected the old man to stand by his side—Drake knew enough about his father not to hope for this—but it had still hurt when his father had discarded him to pick a new heir. When he'd found out, he'd sworn that day to gain control of the company. What he was seeing today was the fruit of his hard labor to make that a reality. It was time for his father to step down and retire. Drake's era had dawned.

"What do you want, Drake?" That was his father, straight to the point with no pleasantries needed.

"I want an additional thirty percent share in Collmark."

His father's cool gaze assessed him. The implications were clear—Drake wanted to be the company's majority shareholder. But he didn't seem surprised by the demand. It was like he'd expected it. "And if I refuse?"

"You can just continue to watch the value of Coll-mark's assets under management drop like they are doing now. And I'll make sure the investors hear about it faster than you can say Jack Robinson."

His father stayed silent. They both knew Drake was behind the events that had brought the company to its current state. But there was no evidence to prove his guilt. Despite how much his father and the employees had tried to figure out what was going on, Drake had been a ghost. His father couldn't afford any more damage to the company and probably couldn't keep its current state secret from his investors for much longer. It would spell the end of the company once investors descended like vultures in their bid to get their money back. And his father couldn't let his legacy and reputation be destroyed just like that. "Done," he said finally.

"Hold on, that's not all." Drake took his sweet time sipping the cup of coffee that was in front of him. It had a bright taste. Perfect, just like the way he was feeling right now. His father's eyes flashed, but he said nothing. "I have two conditions."

"What are they?" his father asked.

"One, you have to retire, effective this evening. The news will go out on the wire tonight." The muscle in his father's jaw twitched, though he remained silent. "Number two, you have to fire Stevie Knox."

"Steven Knox."

"Yeah, whatever. Just take him along with you. I don't want his grubby hands on what belongs to me."

"Anything else?"

"That's it."

His father snapped his fingers, and a man who Drake recognized as his father's long-time lawyer materialized as if out of thin air. Without speaking a word, he opened his briefcase and extracted a set of documents and handed them to his father.

Drake smirked. So his father had known what he wanted.

His old man signed the documents and then handed them to Drake. Drake looked them over and nodded, satisfied that there were no traps hidden in the fine print that could trip him up in the future. He signed both documents and gave one of them back to his father. The lawyer accepted the document from his father and tucked it back in his briefcase before stepping away.

His father didn't utter another word—he just got up and strode out of the restaurant, his wooden walking cane making a *clickety-clack* sound on the tiled floor. Drake had felt the brunt of that cane on his back for many years and wasn't sad to see it go. It was obvious his father had no plans to reunite with him ever again. He could only imagine how much havoc that cane would wreck in the house once his father got home.

Drake had won, but the victory didn't taste as sweet as he had expected. But that didn't matter. Now he could do whatever he liked with the company, and nobody would stand in his way. Phase One of his plan had been successfully completed.

It was time to focus on Phase Two.

———————

Drake whistled to himself as he reclined on the sofa in his old home office. He'd moved back to his original home after the meeting. There had been no need to hide any longer after the discussion with his father. He'd never thought it possible, but he'd missed this place with its fifteen-foot floor-to-ceiling windows. Drake loved the spectacular view of the city from it. It had been the first place he'd bought when he made his first million, and it had surprised him that he had nostalgic memories of his early morning swims in the infinity pool located in the private rooftop terrace.

He inhaled deeply. *Ah, the sweet scent of victory,* he thought. He now had control over his old man's company. And if things went according to plan, he would soon have control over the city. That would be the fulfillment of his long-time dream. But right now, it was time to celebrate. Going to the H Club might do the trick.

A knock sounded on the door. Drake turned his head to see Tiny walk in dressed in his customary black outfit.

His mood turned sour. He hated betrayals no matter how little. Maybe it was time to take care of Tiny too.

"What is it?" he barked.

"I've got news about Zora Smyth. She just got suspended."

Drake rubbed his fingers along his jaw line. "That's not too bad. She can handle it."

"What do you want me to do?"

"Keep an eye on her as always. Any other news?"

"Nothing else."

"Alright. Now, since I've gotten what I want from my father, it's time to disband the team. The Collmark funds need to start making money again."

"Yes, sir."

"You can go." Tiny stepped out of his office.

Drake got up and sauntered over to his desk. He sat down in his swivel chair and opened his desk drawer to pull out the black burner phone. He dialed a number and it went to voicemail. Drake disconnected the call. A few seconds later the phone rang. He picked it up. "Any news on the girl?" he asked.

"She was suspended," Monkey said from the other end of the line.

"Anything else?"

"It seems she may have a new man in her life. A Detective Dave McKesson came to visit her. Turns out her roommate is missing. I looked him up, and he has a history with her—they've dated before."

Drake's jaw tightened. No other man was allowed in Zora's life, no matter who he was. And Tiny had not told him about the detective. A second betrayal.

"What would you like me to do?" Monkey said.

"I need you to confirm that he's actually dating her. Let me know when you find out."

"You got it."

"Did you get any information on the other matter that I asked you to dig into?"

"Not yet, but I'm working on some interesting leads today. I'll likely have some updates for you in a few days."

"I'll need it faster than that."

"I'll do what I can. You don't have to worry. It will be good."

"Alright." The line clicked dead.

Drake placed the phone back in his desk drawer and locked it. He got up from his chair and paced the front of his desk. He stopped and grabbed a paperweight that was on his desk. It was a gift from his father when he'd made his first million and which he'd always kept as a memento. He tossed it from one hand to the other as he walked back and forth.

A new man. Zora didn't have that right. He banged his fist on his desk, and the papers on the surface scattered. She belonged only to him, and if he couldn't have her, no one else could. But he would have to tread carefully if there was a detective hovering around her. There was no need to bring undue attention to himself—he still had his side business to consider.

For now, he would watch and wait.

And if things changed, he would take drastic action.

23

Z ora had tossed and turned all weekend. There'd been no news from Christina—no phone calls or text messages. She had checked in with Dave to see if there'd been any progress on finding her whereabouts. He was still waiting for the results from forensics and had interviewed Christina's colleagues, but nothing had come of it.

His team was still trying to track down Nurse Keller —her sister had confirmed she was on vacation outside the area. Nurse Keller had told her she would be incommunicado for the duration of her vacation to get the rest she needed. And none of the other SICU medical staff who had been on-call that night remembered Christina. Dr. Graham had also been harder to pin down. Dave figured he probably had something to hide and promised to stay on his tail.

Zora had thought about calling Marcus to see if he could help with the case. More eyes on it could only help. But Marcus had gone on an important assignment overseas and would only be back in two weeks' time. Which would be too late for Christina.

The logical next step would have been to call Christina's mother to let her know what was going on. But Zora was nervous about doing so. Christina's mom had had a series of heart attacks last year and was only now getting back to good health. Telling her about Christina would set her back. But then Christina was her only child, and if Zora was in her mom's shoes she would want to be told the truth. But knowing Christina, she would not have wanted her mom to know what was going on. That put Zora in a conundrum. So she decided not to tell her unless she had some positive progress news to report as well—or if it became inevitable, which was an option Zora refused to consider.

The disciplinary interview at ten a.m. that Monday morning had also weighed heavily on her mind as she headed to the hospital. Zora had prepped for the interview, but in hindsight she shouldn't have invested the effort.

The interview had been a disaster. From the moment she'd stepped into the conference room, the interview had pretty much been taken out of her hands. No one listened to anything she had to say. The committee had droned on and on, finishing each other's sentences as if they had rehearsed together beforehand. The whole thing smelled of a setup. She didn't get why they'd even bothered calling her in. She supposed they wanted to be able to note that they had done everything by the book.

She was seeing one of her patients when she got the notice about their decision. Zora was suspended for a full month. The ad hoc committee notified her they would forward their report to the Medical Executive Committee, who could accept, reject, or modify the recommendations. The final decision from MEC would be sent to her by certified mail. At that time, she could exercise her right to a judicial review hearing. But Zora sensed this was merely a formality to fend off any future lawsuits and convince themselves that they had carried out a fair process before firing her. And if she didn't resolve this case against her and stop the process, she might even end up losing everything, even her medical license.

Zora tried to maintain a straight face and a cool head as she saw her remaining patients. She could feel eyes on her back as she moved from one patient to the next; she was sure the other medical staff had already heard the news. The hospital grapevine never slept and was as efficient as ever in spreading gossip around the hospital. But this was her first time as a victim of the vicious network.

She handed over her patients to the attending-on-duty. He remained solemn, unlike his usual cheerful self, as she discussed the patients with him. But she didn't need the pity. She was dying to get out of the hospital, but she needed to first make sure that her patients were in good hands.

Zora held herself ramrod straight as she left the acute care general surgical unit and headed to the call room to pick her things. The room was empty save for a junior resident in a corner, who pretended to be reading and refused to look her in the eye. It was just as well. She wasn't in the mood for chitchat. She was about to press the code to open her locker when she noticed that the locker's door was slightly ajar. Zora jerked the door open, and her items spilled out onto the floor.

Her heart picked up its pace. Someone had been to her locker. She usually kept everything in its own place, since it made it easier for her to find whatever she was looking for.

She turned to the junior resident. "Did anyone come to my locker?" she asked.

The junior resident ignored her.

"Taylor, I asked you a question."

Taylor looked up from the book he was holding and stared brazenly into her eyes. "I don't know," he said.

The insolent twat. So he'd heard her the first time. He must be gloating about her situation since she'd embarrassed him last week when he'd almost killed a patient with his incompetence. *Well, enjoy it while it lasts because I'll be back and on your case,* she thought.

Zora turned back to her locker and picked up her items from the floor. What could they have been searching for? And then she remembered. She dug into the back of her locker and pulled out the ASCRS Textbook of Colon and Rectal Surgery that she kept at the bottom. She flipped through the book, but she couldn't find the copy of Jane Doe's operative report that she'd stuffed there. She turned the book upside down and shook its pages. Nothing fell out. It was gone.

Zora dropped the book back in her locker and leaned her head against its door. So they had wanted to erase every trace of Jane Doe's records. But they hadn't known she would take precautionary measures. They had no idea she had stored an electronic copy of the report in a cloud account, and the attending had backed up his files elsewhere. They must be dreaming if they thought they had bested her.

She grabbed her bag from her locker and slammed the door shut. From the corner of her eye, she spotted the resident sending a text on his phone as she left the room. Probably providing the grapevine with latest update on Zora celebrity news.

On her way out of the hospital, Zora could hear the murmurings. She gritted her teeth and kept her gaze straight ahead. From the corner of her eye, she saw nurses she'd worked with averting their eyes, a few residents from other departments who pointed her out to their colleagues, and non-medical staff who pushed their carts further away when they passed her. It was like she was suddenly a leper, and nobody wanted to get infected.

She tried to think logically and told herself that a good majority of the medical staff were people like her, who were much more focused on helping the sick than discussing the latest gossip, and so were probably attending to their patients. But her heart wished they were here instead to cheer her on.

Zora exited the hospital and hailed a cab from the cab zone. The sound of thunder clapped loudly against her ears as she rode home. The skies threatened a downpour, black clouds skirting the horizon. It was as if the whole universe agreed with the verdict against her.

The ride to her apartment was quick. She lumbered up the stairs and opened her apartment door. The place seemed empty, devoid of life. Zora wondered if the brightness she had always felt on entering her home had been a dream. An optical illusion.

She dropped her bag on the couch and looked at the living room corner to see if she needed to water her favorite plant, the hardy one among the others. But it was dead. Dead like her life.

That was when the sobs swelled within her and broke through. Zora's tears flowed as she collapsed on the couch, and the sobs racked her body. She didn't know how long she stayed in that position.

When she opened her eyes, it was dark outside the windows. Zora sat up and rubbed her puffy eyes. She had cried herself to sleep.

Everything that had happened came flooding back as she sat there staring into space. Had it really been only about a week ago that John Doe disappeared? One minute she had been a witness reporting a case, and now she was the victim in yet another witch hunt. Why her and not someone else? Not that she wished this on anyone. But she'd been minding her own business, focused solely on saving patients' lives.

There was no reason why this should be happening to her.

But she couldn't change what had happened. There was only one thing to do. She was going to fight back. They had another thing coming if they thought she was just going to wilt and die.

But first she had to eat something, even if she wasn't really hungry. Zora got up, padded across the living room to the kitchen, and opened her stainless-steel fridge. It was empty save for a half-full bottle of milk, which smelled rancid. Zora tossed the bottle in the garbage can under her sink.

She searched the cupboards and found a packet of popcorn. It would do for now. Cooking had never been her strong suit, so she had learned to stock only the basic necessities. Popcorn was one of them. Christina was the cook; she loved making dishes from all over the world. Christina. Tears welled up behind Zora's eyes at the thought of her. *Hang in there, Christina. We'll find you*, she thought.

Zora sniffled as she popped the popcorn pack into the microwave. This was not the time for tears. A few minutes later, the microwave dinged. Zora removed the popcorn, poured it into a clean bowl, and carried it back to the living room.

She needed to get a good handle on her emotions,

and then the planning could begin. The only way was to distract herself. So she picked up the remote control from a side table. As she flipped through the channels, nothing caught her attention. She didn't feel like watching the romantic comedy on Channel Five, and the medical drama on Channel Twelve only amplified her pain.

As she changed the channels randomly, a news headline caught her attention. Zora dropped the remote on the coffee table and leaned closer to hear what the reporter was saying. A body had been found in the nearby reservoir, and the police had just identified the body.

Zora gasped.

24

The picture that stared back at her was Jane Doe! Her name was Jasmine, and she had been a student at the local college. Zora's heart quickened and she barely held back her excitement. This was the patient that everyone had claimed didn't exist! As Zora watched, she discovered Jasmine had a family.

That was when she remembered the man. The one she had bumped into on her way into the ER. The man that had claimed that he was Jasmine's brother. Zora was skeptical of the relationship; the man looked like a bouncer, unlike Jasmine, who had more delicate features. And he had disappeared. A real brother would never have abandoned his sister in the ER just like that.

Zora's mind raced, and she stood up and paced.

Though it was a terrible loss of life, Zora finally had good lead—her sail had finally caught new wind.

Time to find out more. The reporter had mentioned that an autopsy had been done and the body released to the family. The family wanted to bury her immediately, so the funeral service was scheduled for tomorrow. Which meant that the man would be in attendance if he was really Jasmine's brother. But her instincts told her that wasn't the case. Which meant he might be involved in her death; he didn't seem a Good Samaritan type of fellow. Tracking him down might give her a clue as to who had set her up.

Maybe she should call Dave and let him know. Zora stopped pacing. No, she needed to be sure first before reaching out to him.

Her next step was now clear—she would attend the funeral service. The reporter had stated that it was scheduled for ten a.m. Nothing was going to keep her away.

She would start there.

25

Zora entered the church. It was a small Catholic church on the outskirts of town. She'd passed the steepled church building a time or two before, so it had been relatively easy to find. A large crucifix on the wall was the first thing she saw as she oriented herself to the church's interior layout.

Rows of pews extended on either side from the front of the church to the back where she stood. The church's dark stained-glass windows muted the light that streamed into the church's interior and masked its gothic architecture. The space seemed empty save for a few people seated on the front pew on the left. A lectern stood on a raised platform in front of the large crucifix and faced the rest of the sanctuary. On its right, a closed white casket rested on a table.

Zora slipped into one of the pews in the back and watched the service. Wearing a cream-colored top and tan skirt, she blended easily into the background. An elderly priest ministered to an old woman who sat next to a boy of about fourteen years. A middle-aged couple dressed in matching grey suits sat with them. Probably relatives or family friends of the grey-haired lady.

Zora couldn't see the bouncer guy anywhere. If he was truly Jasmine's brother, he would have been here. While she mused about it, someone slipped in beside her and she started. She turned to see who it was, and her eyes widened. "What are you doing here?" she whispered.

"What are you doing here?" Dave asked pointedly, ignoring the question.

"This was the patient I was telling you about, Jane Doe."

"You mean ..."

"Yes, the one with the missing kidney that disappeared."

"Why didn't you tell me?"

"I just found out on the news yesterday and I planned to inform you after I found out a bit more from attending this funeral. But I didn't know you were in charge of this investigation," Zora retorted.

"So, what have you learned?"

Zora looked toward the front of the church to see the priest praying for the family. "At the ER, there was a man who claimed to be her brother. He abandoned her there and disappeared. I figured if he was the brother, he would be here at the funeral. But he is not. Shouldn't it be a given that he be here if they were that closely related?"

Dave stayed quiet for a moment. "Can you still remember what he looked like?"

"I suppose so."

Dave chuckled. "You still have your way with words. A simple yes would have worked. Why don't you come with me to the station and I'll ask our forensic artist to sketch out this guy? He might already be in our system."

"No."

"What do you mean, no?" he said, his voice a little louder than necessary. The priest looked in their direction.

"Shh, you are disturbing the funeral!"

"Okay, okay." Dave lowered his voice to a whisper. "Why not?"

"I'm allergic to the police station."

Dave burst out laughing. The priest looked up and gave them a stern look. Dave gave him an apologetic smile in return. Zora ducked her head. Dave was going to be the death of her.

"What does that even mean?" he whispered. Zora stayed silent and looked ahead. "Okay. Would a café near the station work?"

"That's fine."

Dave looked at her in silence for a few seconds. "I'll call the guy and set it up."

"Yes, that looks like the guy. That's all I can remember." She leaned back on the chair and folded her arms across her chest. She was happy she'd been able to recall most of his features, and the sketch seemed a close likeness to the man she had seen.

"I'll run it through the system and get back to you, Dave," the sketch artist said. He stood up as he put his tablet back into his bag.

"Thank you. Let me know as soon as you find out," Dave responded. The sketch artist nodded, picked his bag, and left the cafe.

Zora looked around the room. The smell of coffee and cinnamon hung heavy in the air. The cafe looked like it had seen better days; its wallpaper was old, tired, and worn in some spots. The table Zora sat at had scratches all over its top, and some of the chairs were mismatched. But the coffee and pastries were surprisingly good. The place was empty save for a few customers, one who was reading a newspaper and the other working from his laptop. Neither seemed to pay any attention to her.

"You did good," Dave said.

"It's not a big deal. Doctors have strong powers of observation. It's what makes us good at what we do." Zora took a sip of her coffee and looked out of the window. She could see the police station across the street. The place gave her the heebie-jeebies and brought back memories she didn't want. Zora shuddered and fiddled with the pendant around her neck.

She turned back to Dave. "Do you have any updates on Christina's whereabouts?" she asked.

"I should hear back from forensics tomorrow," Dave responded. "We are still trying to track down the SICU nurse. It turns out she went on a cruise, but we are not sure which. Hopefully, we'll find out more soon."

"Did I tell you that my locker was ransacked, and Jasmine's operative report disappeared?"

Dave leaned forward, his brows furrowed in a

frown. "Who knew about the report?"

"Only everyone on the ad hoc committee which probably meant the whole hospital leadership."

"So that's gone. It's alright though. We'll find more evidence."

"Nope, we are good. They don't know I saved a copy of the report on the cloud. And the attending secured his too."

"That's my girl!" Dave realized what he had said, and his face heated up. "Sorry."

Zora chuckled. "No worries. I'll make sure it stays safe till we need it."

Zora felt eyes on her back and she turned around. She caught the man with the newspaper duck his head. Had he been watching her? She stared at him, but he kept his eyes on the paper in front of him. Maybe she was just being paranoid after her experience with the hospital gossip.

"What is it?" Dave turned his head to see what she was looking at.

"I don't know. It's probably nothing."

"Are you sure?"

Zora looked at Dave. "Yes." She finished her drink. "I think I should get going. Let me know if you find out anything else about the case." She downed her remaining coffee and got up.

"Don't worry, we'll handle everything. And Zora?"

"Hmmm?" Zora looked down at Dave.

"It will be okay. We'll find Christina," Dave said in a calming voice.

Zora exhaled. "Thank you." She gave him a small smile.

Dave returned her smile but said nothing.

Zora picked up her bag from the chair next to where she'd sat and left for home.

———

Zora sank into her sofa and dropped her bag beside her. Sunlight streamed in from the open curtains. She was tired, but it had been a productive day. She'd been scared when Dave sat next to her at the church. For a minute, she had been afraid that it might be someone working for whoever was behind everything. Dave had no idea how relieved she'd been to see him. No criminal in his right mind would have tried to approach her with a detective around. And they would have known Dave was one. He had the *look*.

Zora propped her legs on the coffee table. The traffic on her way back had been horrendous—a triple car accident had completely blocked the roads—so the trip had taken several hours instead of minutes. She leaned back on the sofa. She couldn't wait to take a soak in the bathtub. It would help in washing away the ickiness she'd felt from being close to the police station. Zora pulled off the hair tie holding her ponytail together and ran her hand through her hair.

Her phone rang at that moment. Who could it be? Her pulse quickened. Maybe it was news about Christina. Zora opened her bag and retrieved her phone. She frowned when she saw the number on the screen. Stewart. Why was he calling her? She wasn't really in the mood to speak with anyone from the hospital. *Be nice, Zora. He helped you look for Christina,* she thought. Zora pressed the green button. "This is Dr. Smyth."

"Zora, it's Stewart. I heard about what happened— the suspension, I mean. Are you okay?"

Zora shifted on the couch. "I'm good."

"Well, I wanted you to know that I believe you. And I've told our colleagues that you did nothing wrong. There must be something going on. I'll keep digging around here to see what I can find."

She crossed and uncrossed her legs. "You don't have to. I wouldn't want you to put yourself in harm's way."

"It's no problem. I'll be very discreet."

"In that case, thank you. That would be helpful."

"It's nothing. Have you found Christina?"

Zora felt a stab of pain in her chest. There'd been no progress on Christina's whereabouts. With each passing day, the chance of finding Christina alive was getting slimmer. "Not yet."

"I'm sure you'll find her soon."

She let out a small sigh. "Thank you."

"I'll call you later if I hear anything."

"Thanks. Bye." The call disconnected from the other end of the line.

Zora tossed her phone on the couch and leaned back. One more person who believed her. Truth be told, she'd been hurt by how folks at the hospital—people she had worked closely with for over four years—had easily believed the lies about her. Only Brian had reached out to find out how she was doing. And now Stewart. She wouldn't forget his act of kindness.

Her phone buzzed again. Zora turned her head to look at the screen. It was a number she didn't know. Was it about Christina? She sat up and pressed the answer button. "This is Zora," she said.

"Zora, it's me, Dave."

Zora leaned forward. "Is something wrong? Is it news about Christina?"

"No, it's not. It's about Jasmine. The case has just been ruled a suicide."

Fifteen minutes later, Dave sat across Zora at a local gourmet coffee shop near her house. He nursed a cup of coffee that Zora had ordered on his behalf as soon as she'd arrived. The cafe had a cool vibe— with its simple pale green and chocolate brown decor, the smell of freshly ground coffee mixed with fresh homemade bread, the comfortable chairs set in nooks, and the large windows that filled the space with natural light. But it did nothing for her today.

"What happened?" Zora asked.

Dave rubbed the back of his neck. "First things first. I heard back from the sketch artist. It turns out our guy is Vadim Pavlishchev, a.k.a. Thunder, one of the top members of an Eastern European crime group, suspected to be involved in racketeering, prostitution, murder, you name it. But they've never been caught and have always managed to slip through the dragnet. The only reason we have his details is because he is a suspect in another case. We are dealing with some very bad guys here, Zora."

Zora fingered her pendant and digested the information. This was beyond the scope of what she'd thought. Organized crime was a very different world than the one she lived in. She shivered. "But what would Jasmine have in common with him? She was a decent girl going to college. I can't imagine how their paths would have crossed. And she's not of East European descent."

Dave rested his elbows on the table. "That's what I can't figure out. Anyway, I took the information to the chief. Imagine my shock when he told me that the case had been ruled a suicide and ordered me to close it. When I protested, he advised me to let it go. That there was pressure from above to close the case. And there was no evidence of foul play—a suicide note was even found in her pocket, which the handwriting experts have confirmed to be hers. In his words, 'Hearsay from a random witness is not enough to keep this case open.'"

Zora's nostrils flared. She was not a random witness, and the police chief had no right to ridicule her. This was yet another reason why she disliked the police. "So have you closed the case?"

Dave's hands played with the coffee mug. "I had no choice. I still plan to investigate informally. But I feel uneasy about you poking your head into this case. These guys are a mean bunch, and I wouldn't want anything bad to happen to you. Something tells me we might end up rattling the hornet's nest. I don't want to see you hurt."

Heat radiated through Zora's chest at Dave's words. She appreciated his words, more than he would ever know. But this was her fight, and she wasn't backing down, no matter how scary everything now seemed.

She lifted her cup of coffee to her lips and took a sip. There was nothing wrong with the coffee as far as she could tell, but for some reason it tasted flat today. She laid the cup back on the table and leaned back on her chair. "Thanks for looking out for me, but I have to do this. I need to get my life back, and it seems to be tied to this case."

Dave sighed. "I had a feeling you might say that." He pulled an object from his pocket and held it out to her. It was a small nondescript black phone. "This is an unregistered number. I'll only call you on this line and vice versa. Since this case might have some high-level connections, there is a possibility that we are being watched, and your line may have been tapped. I'd prefer to err on the side of caution and make sure you stay safe. On the other hand, Christina's case is still officially open, so I'll continue to pursue leads on that front."

"Thanks." Zora took the phone and dropped it into her bag.

"So what are you planning to do next?" Dave asked.

"Since I've been suspended and have all this free time on my hands, I'm going to continue to work my hospital connections to see if there's anyone who knows exactly where Nurse Keller travelled to. I'm sure she must have interacted with Christina, since they had both assured me they'll be able to watch over Jasmine that morning. Don't worry, I'll be careful."

"Okay. I'll continue to work it from my end as well," Dave said. "We might have found a way to crack Dr. Graham." The mere mention of Graham's name brought bile to Zora's mouth. "I'll let you know once it's done."

"Sounds good." Zora finished off her coffee.

Dave looked at his watch. "I have to go. Why don't I drop you off?"

Zora waved him away. "It's only a five-minute walk. I'm fine. Go."

"Be careful, alright?" he said softly as his eyes

searched Zora's face. Her skin tingled, and her stomach fluttered at the sound of his voice.

"Yes, I will," she replied with a smile.

Dave squeezed her shoulder as he walked past, and then he left.

Zora leaned back, and the smile disappeared from her face. If Zora was truthful with herself, she was a little scared since she was treading on unchartered territory. The cartel business was not really her thing. But Zora was going to charge ahead like she always did.

Because Christina needed her. And Zora wanted her life back.

She had never run from a challenge, and she wasn't planning to start now.

27

Drake's eyes flickered open at the incessant ringing that pounded inside his head like a jackhammer. He didn't know when he'd fallen asleep in his home office. It had been a long night, and he had just finished a remote forty-eight-hour working session with the Collmark strategy team. They had planned and executed trading strategies that would shore up Collmark's funds. The team had made significant progress, and Drake had given them some time off to go home and freshen up before they started all over again. He'd planned to take care of some urgent administrative work. But he'd been too exhausted and had dozed off at his desk instead.

The phone kept ringing. It had to be Monkey. Maybe he'd gotten the information Drake wanted.

Drake had given him strict instructions to only call when he had important news to deliver.

He raised his head and opened the desk drawer to pick up the black burner phone. Drake pressed the right button and held the phone against his ear.

"I have news about Zora and the detective," Monkey wasted no time in saying. "They met again at a coffee shop today. I couldn't hear what they were saying from where I sat, but it was obvious that they are more than friends."

Drake's throat went dry, and his vision clouded. He gripped the familiar paperweight on his desk. Zora belonged to him. She had no right to think about another guy.

"Are you sure?" Drake asked.

"Positive. What would you like me to do?"

"Take care of her. Make sure it's so clean that no one can figure out what happened. We don't want the detective tracing it back to us."

"Will do." The line went dead.

Drake dropped the phone back in the desk drawer. He examined the paperweight in his hand. It was a beautiful piece of work, and he had enjoyed admiring it every morning. Such a shame. He threw it across the room, and it hit the opposite wall and smashed into pieces.

Since Zora had crossed the line, she had to pay the price. He would miss her. But there was nothing to be done about that.

She was better off dead than dallying with another man.

28

The man took a final look over the surgical tools displayed on the instrument table. He had everything he needed. His lips twitched as he touched each instrument with his gloved hand, knowing he was going to use it to deliver what he'd promised, be it life or death.

The metal doors slid open, and Erik walked in. The man's eyes narrowed. He hated interruptions when he was going through this important ritual. Erik was lucky that the man had just finished, otherwise he would have been punished. He didn't tolerate disobedience from the people that worked for him. It was the most important lesson his father had taught him. "What is it?" the man asked.

"I'm sorry, boss. It's Monkey. Mr. Pierce has given

him the order to kill Dr. Smyth. He wants to know what you want him to do."

The man frowned. "Why?"

"Monkey says Mr. Pierce found out Detective Dave and Dr. Smyth have something going on between them."

The muscle in the man's jaw flickered. He knew Drake was obsessed with Zora, but by ordering her death he'd practically gone off the deep end and clearly wasn't thinking. Killing Zora now would be messy and could draw more attention to their business. It was a good thing that the police had no idea of Drake's involvement in the profitable enterprise. Maybe it was best to take care of him now before he became a problem.

"Boss, what would you like him to do?"

"Tell him to leave Zora alone. But it's time to take care of Pierce."

"Yes, boss." Erik pivoted and left the room.

Drake Pierce. *Goodbye to utter rubbish,* he thought. The best thing was that no one would miss him, not even his old man.

He checked the time on the wall clock, and an adrenaline rush filled his veins. The next human painting would be here soon.

He could hardly wait.

29

Tiny removed his wireless headphones and laid them on the kitchen counter. He'd been preparing Drake's lunch when the call from Monkey came in. Drake didn't like eating out except when it was necessary. So Tiny had learned how to cook.

Tiny knew all about Monkey and the conversations he'd had with Drake. He had decided long ago that he needed some insurance policy, since working with Drake was such a high-risk job. If he wasn't careful, he could be left holding the bag if things went wrong. So he'd installed spyware on Drake's burner phones that activated when a call was placed. Tiny could now record them, and Drake was none the wiser. The files could come in handy in the future.

Tiny had no illusions about Drake's loyalty, even though he'd worked with Drake for many years. Drake was committed only to himself, everyone else was either supposed to be used or disposed of. And Tiny had no plans to end up at the bottom of the river.

And now he'd just found out that Drake had put out a hit on Zora. Drake had always assumed that Tiny had a thing for her, but it wasn't in the way Drake thought. Zora reminded Tiny of his younger sister, who had been killed by a gangbanger. She had been smart, an honor student who had looked forward to attending college away from the streets they had grown up in. She had planned to become a doctor.

But on the eve of her graduation from high school, she'd been gunned down on her way back from the grocery store. The gang members in question had later claimed that they'd thought she was someone else. But that didn't matter to Tiny. Justice had to be served, and he had taken three lives for the one that was lost. He'd been caught and had ended up with murder charges with a possible life sentence. But he had crossed paths with Drake in the courthouse, and Drake had taken an interest in him and managed the impossible feat of getting him off as a free man. And Tiny had pledged to work under him.

But he hadn't known that under all Drake's

geniality existed a brutal sociopath. Tiny had sold his soul to the devil. He had ended up killing more people under Drake's orders than he cared to remember. The only thing that kept him sane through it all was thinking about his sister. But then memories of her face had started fading. Then he'd met Zora, and it was as if his sister was standing alive in front of him.

Tiny was aware Zora was a different person from his sister. But getting updates on her had become the one bright spot in his dreary life, and watching over her had been like a chance at redemption. And now Drake wanted to take everything away.

He couldn't let that happen no matter what.

It was time to intervene, and he had to do it quickly.

30

The black phone rang from her bedside table. Zora lifted her head despite feeling groggy and looked at the alarm clock beside it. It was only one a.m. Why was Dave calling her so early, especially after she'd met him at the cafe just a few hours ago? She picked up the phone and answered it. "Hello."

"It's me. Dave." Zora heard what sounded like shuffling of papers in the background. "Do you think you could come to the station now? I know you would prefer not to, but it's about the case. You might want to witness this conversation that's about to take place."

Sleep fled Zora's eyes, and she sat up. She hated stepping into the police station, but solving this case was top priority. She took a deep breath. She could do this. "Sure, I can be there in fifteen minutes."

"Good. Call me when you get here." He disconnected the call.

Zora scrambled out of bed, called a taxi service, and dressed quickly in jeans and black jacket over a blue V-neck T-shirt. By the time she'd descended to the bottom of the stairs, a cab was waiting for her in front of the building. Zora jumped in and urged the cab driver to head to the station. She called Dave as she arrived, and he met her outside.

He didn't bother with pleasantries. "Let's head to the interrogation room," he said. "We'll talk once we get there." Dave turned and led the way into the station. Zora's heart flipped over, but she steeled herself and followed him inside. If she didn't know any better, she would have thought she was a suspect from the brusque way Dave spoke to her.

The police station hadn't changed much from the last time she'd been there, but everything seemed different somehow. Even though she'd rather be anywhere else, she didn't feel the usual urge to flee the station. Of course the smell of aged coffee, stale pizza, and something acrid she couldn't name assaulted her nostrils as they passed the break room. There were only a few people in the main area of the station, and they were either busy with their heads down, talking into phones, or taking naps. None of them paid Zora any attention.

Zora didn't expect to see any familiar faces. She'd heard from Marcus a few years ago that Detective Morris had moved out of state and was now working for the New Jersey Police Department. His partner—Detective Shepherd—had been medically retired due to injuries he had sustained on the job.

Dave led her down the hallway to a grey door and stepped in. Zora slipped in after him into a small narrow room with a large two-way mirror positioned about five feet high on one side of the wall. A counter with two computer monitors on it ran below the full width of the mirror. Zora could see through into an interrogation room.

Graham was sprawled in a chair behind a table bolted down in the center of the room, his goatee unkempt and his tie askew. Zora could also see CCTV cameras mounted in the upper corners of the interrogation room, their videos captured on the computer monitors in front of her. *So this is how it looks like from the other side of the room*, she thought.

Dave moved closer to where she stood. The woody smell of his cologne wafted up her nostrils, and she resisted the urge to lean in. It seemed some things never changed.

"I'm sorry about the way I brought you in. I needed to get you in here as fast as possible without any witnesses. How are you feeling?" Dave asked, his eyes searching her face.

"Good." Well, more than good if he kept standing this close to her.

Dave turned back to the mirror. "We've just arrested Dr. Graham for illegal gambling," he said. "Since it's not looking great for him, I figured this might be the best time to ask him some questions regarding Jasmine's case. I think we can shake something loose from him before his lawyer arrives, and I thought you might want to listen to whatever he has to say. Why don't you wait here while I go talk to him?"

Zora nodded, keeping her face impassive. Even though the idea of being alone in a room in the police station brought back memories she'd prefer to stay buried, she would not think about them. She had to focus on what was about to happen in the next several minutes.

Dave left the observation room and shut the door behind him.

Zora crossed her arms around herself and watched Dave enter the interrogation room a few seconds later with a burly cop in tow. He sat opposite Dr. Graham, while the other cop stood in a corner of the room.

"Dr. Ronald Graham, I'm Detective Dave McKesson, and this is my partner." Dave gestured at the cop in the corner. "Like you were told earlier, you've been arrested and charged with illegal gambling. You are aware that you have the right to remain silent and to refuse to answer questions, anything you say may be used against you in a court of law, you have the right to consult an attorney before speaking to the police, and to have an attorney present during questioning now or in the future. If you cannot afford an attorney, one will be appointed for you before any questioning if you wish, and if you decide to answer questions now without an attorney present, you still have the right to stop answering at any time until you talk to an attorney."

Zora saw Graham sit up in his chair. "I want my lawyer. I'm not talking till he gets here," he said.

"Sure. We'll just wait right here till he comes. In the meantime, let me help you understand what's going to happen to you."

Dr. Graham stayed silent, but seemed to be listening.

"Since we caught you in the act and have the evidence to prove you were involved in illegal gambling, we expect that you'll be convicted and get up to one year in jail. Which means you will lose your medical license."

Zora lifted an eyebrow. Dave had just stretched the truth. Even though a doctor in this state would get his license revoked with a felony conviction—since it constituted unprofessional misconduct—such revocations were not permanent. Those would only happen in felony cases such as murder, rape, and assault, financial crimes such as extortion, embezzlement, and income tax evasion, criminal neglect or misconduct resulting from patient care, and drug use and narcotic diversion.

Graham could appeal to have his medical license reinstated once he'd completed his sentence, even though the process was typically lengthy and laborious. But Graham didn't know that. His eyes widened, though he fought to hide his alarm.

Zora leaned forward, all her nervousness forgotten. She hated lying as an interrogation tactic, but she hoped it would work in this case.

Dave's eyes stayed fixed on Graham's face. "That means all those years you've invested in becoming a doctor? Poof. Gone, just like that," Dave said.

Dr. Graham swallowed. "You're lying."

Dave leaned in. "You think so?"

Dr. Graham's laryngeal prominence bobbed again. "I want a deal."

"A deal? With what?"

"I know something that might be helpful to you."

Dave stared back at him. "Go on."

"It's for a very important case. I'll tell you everything as long as I don't get taped. And I get no jail time."

"It depends on what you tell me."

Dr. Graham went on to tell Dave that it had all started last year when his mom fell sick and needed a coronary bypass. Her insurance wouldn't cover it, and he had a lot of student loans that still needed to be paid off. Some friends of his had invited him to a club, promising him that he could make a lot of money in an easy straightforward way. All he needed to do was roll some dice, and since he was a brilliant doctor, he could put his analytical skills to good use. Graham was desperate, so he'd followed along and taken the chance.

But luck wasn't on his side and he'd ended up in more debt. His new creditors didn't waste any time in coming after him. They told him the only way to write off the debt was for him to assist with certain surgeries they had in mind. It wouldn't really be anything illegal, and they would also pay him extra to make it worthwhile. But if he refused, then he would have to give up his organs as payment. All they needed him to do was take care of the patients brought into the ER without asking any questions.

The choice had been clear for him. He'd acquiesced on the condition that they also pay for his mother's surgery. Since then, they'd brought in patients for him and he'd made enough money that his total debt was almost paid off. He'd also never seen any of the patients again after surgery. But that had changed with Jasmine; he'd seen the news about her death. That was why he had gone to the club—to clear his head.

"How many patients are we talking about?" Dave asked.

"I've personally attended to over fifty of them. But I think there might have been more. I don't think I'm the only doctor they use."

Zora's mouth fell open. That would mean about one patient per week at a minimum.

"Any clues to who the other doctors are?"

The door to the interrogation room opened, and a tall man in an expensive tailored suit strode in, holding a briefcase. He was the kind of lawyer that was definitely above Graham's pay grade. "My client is advised not to say another word." He opened his briefcase and handed Dave some papers. "We applied for bail, and my client has been released on his own recognizance."

Wow, that was fast, Zora thought.

"I believe my client is free to leave at this time," the lawyer continued.

Dave said nothing.

The lawyer turned to Graham. "Let's go."

The door to the observation room opened, and Dave walked back in. He shut the door behind him and leaned against the wall.

"What did you think?" Dave asked Zora.

"This feels like something straight out of a movie. Over fifty patients? That's a large number!" Zora said.

"And there may be more."

Zora perched at the edge of the counter and folded her arms across her chest. "For that many patients, there has to be someone higher up in the hospital that is covering for them. Someone with significant authorization to be able to take care of the records and give an unknown operating team access to the OR. I won't be surprised if this is a more complicated network than we imagined."

"I agree."

"So what's next?"

"I plan to check in on Dr. Graham tomorrow to see

what else I can get out of him, but I doubt I'll learn anything new. I know that lawyer. He is one of the heavy hitters in town. I can't even see how Dr. Graham could afford him."

"Maybe someone hired the lawyer on his behalf."

"Most likely. And this lawyer is so good that he'll be able to make the illegal gambling charge go away."

"What if the lawyer works for the cartel? I immediately thought of them when Graham was talking about the creditors. It sounds like something in their wheelhouse."

"That crossed my mind as well. I already plan to look into it."

"Any news about Christina?"

"No new information yet. Forensics didn't find anything—the guys who tossed her room knew what they were doing. We checked her financial records, but there've been no credit card charges or cash withdrawals in recent times. Because we believe Christina's disappearance might be linked in some way to Thunder, we have a few of our informants watching out for him, but there's been no news yet. It's like he's gone underground. But we'll keep looking."

"Thank you." Zora said. She sighed. "Maybe it's time I let Christina's mom know what's going on since it's been a few days since she's disappeared, even if we don't have any new information to share with her. I'll give her a call later today." Zora couldn't help but yawn, and she covered her mouth in embarrassment.

Dave chuckled. "I'd forgotten the time. Let's end it here for now. I also need to get you out of the station before anyone else figures out what we are up to. Why don't I give you a ride home?"

Zora started to shake her head, but then nodded as another yawn escaped from her mouth. "That would be perfect."

Tiny stood outside the frosted glass door that led to Drake's home office. He could hear Drake pacing within, an occasional curse exiting under his breath. Tiny knew what had happened. He'd received an alert when Drake called Monkey. There had been no answer on the other end of the line. And there never would.

Tiny had taken care of Monkey. He had no hard feelings against him; the guy had simply taken the wrong job, an assignment that Tiny could not allow him to complete. The good thing was that Monkey preferred to handle his own jobs instead of outsourcing them, so killing him had closed the assignment from his end. But there was one more loose thread to take care of.

He knocked on the door and heard Drake bark a response. Ordinarily, this would have been a terrible time to see Drake; he could easily transfer all his anger and aggression on Tiny. But time was not on Tiny's side, so he took his chances.

He walked toward the desk and placed the tray he held on its surface. He picked up the glass of water on it and offered it to Drake.

"Thanks," Drake said.

Tiny watched as Drake emptied the glass and handed it back. Tiny placed the glass back on the tray and picked both items to leave the office. As he headed to the door, he heard the sound he was expecting.

Tiny turned to see Drake fall on his knees, his hands clawing at his throat as if to stop what was happening.

"What did you—?" Drake managed to utter.

"I'm sorry, but you shouldn't have tried to kill Zora. Goodbye, Drake." Tiny turned back and left the room.

By the time he came back into the room with a backpack strapped on his back and his hands gloved, he didn't have to look to see what had happened. Drake was dead. And it was time for Tiny to disappear. He'd destroyed the CCTV cameras last night and had already removed all his items from Drake's penthouse, burning whatever he couldn't take along. Luckily, he didn't have much to begin with. To minimize the risk of DNA transfer, he would leave the body where it was for the police to find, whenever that was. Because nobody would miss Drake.

The Collmark strategy team would assume that he was taking some time off and would only inform his father after a few days. By then, Tiny would be very far away, and he already had an alibi in place. He wiped down the surfaces he might have touched, which included the door handles. He'd already disposed of the tray and the glass.

Tiny took one more look at Drake before leaving the room and shutting the door behind him for the final time.

32

The man entered his home and dropped his satchel on the enormous couch in the living room. His family was out but would be back later in the day. He could enjoy some peace and quiet before the place became boisterous again. He kicked off his shoes. It had been a long day at work, and coupled with the side business, he was running on very little sleep. A nap would be nice right about now.

His phone rang and he growled. Who had the guts to disturb him? He pulled it from his pocket and saw that it was Erik. "What is it?" he barked.

"Boss, it's Monkey. He's dead."

The man sat up. "What happened?"

"They said he was killed by a man with tree-like limbs."

"Tiny."

"Yes."

The man rubbed his jaw. "It's best this way. We would have gotten rid of Monkey sooner or later. He knew too much. What about Pierce? Did Monkey take care of him?"

"Mr. Pierce is dead, but he was killed by Tiny."

"Interesting."

"What do you want me to do about him?"

"Leave Tiny alone for now, but keep an eye on him. We can always plant his DNA as evidence and make him the fall guy if we need to. After all, he murdered them both."

"Will do, boss."

33

The sun streaked into Zora's room as she opened her eyes. She looked at the time. It was ten a.m., later than she had ever woken up. Maybe her body was trying to make up for the loss of sleep she had suffered recently from her hectic call schedule. All her synapses were firing better now—a much better state of mind in which to call Christina's mom.

Zora had thought about what she would tell her, but she'd figured the truth was best despite her concerns on how the news would affect her heart. She would make the call in the afternoon. Christina's mom spent her mornings in her garden—for tranquility, Christina had said. Her mom would need it today before receiving the news about Christina.

Zora pulled her phone from under her pillow and noticed she had a new voicemail. It was from Brian, telling her to call him back immediately. She would return the call, but she needed her morning boost first.

Zora rose and ambled to the kitchen. This was the one ritual she allowed herself each morning—making her own fresh coffee. She lifted her bag of Ethopian Yergacheffe coffee beans from its corner of the kitchen countertop, measured out half a cup, ground it in her burr grinder, and poured the grounds into her beloved French press. The press had been a favorite of her father's, and she had inherited it. Once her water had boiled and then cooled for a minute, Zora poured it into the French press and stirred the mixture vigorously. She let it steep for about four minutes, and then plunged the press. Perfect.

The aromatic blend of florals, tangerine, and toasted coconut filled the apartment as she poured the coffee into a mug. Zora inhaled deeply. The scent always had a calming effect on her before she began her day.

With her coffee in hand, Zora settled into the couch and dialed Brian's number. "What's up, Brian?"

"You seem to be enjoying this time off, sleeping late and all," Brian's voice drawled over the line.

Zora leaned back into the couch. It was good to

hear his voice. Brian always had her back. It was an understatement to say that he made the residency program interesting. No one could keep up with his antics. And no one had ever managed to get under his skin. "Why do you think so?"

"I can hear it in your voice, silly."

The corners of her mouth twitched, and Zora shook her head. Brian had it all wrong. "Did anything happen?" she asked. Brian wouldn't be calling back unless he had important news for her.

"I just heard that Dr. Graham left this morning for an exchange program in London."

Zora sat up. "Where did you hear this?"

"The news is all over the hospital. And guess what?"

"What?"

"He is Dr. Anderson's nephew."

Zora set her mug on the coffee table in front of her. "Unbelievable!"

"My dear, you better believe it. Hold on for a second."

Zora heard some indistinct talking in the background.

Brian came back on the call. "Zora honey, let me call you back later, okay?" He disconnected the call.

Zora dropped her phone on the coffee table and studied the table intently for a moment.

Then she got up, walked over to her bedroom, picked up the black phone from the bedside table, and dialed Dave's number. He answered on the second ring.

"Dave, it's Zora. Have you heard that Dr. Graham left the country?"

"Yes, I just found out. I saw he wasn't at home, so I came to the hospital to look for him, and that's when I heard the news. I had him on the no-fly list, so I wonder how he managed to leave the country."

"Someone must have pulled some serious strings. It's also possible he may have left the country using a private jet, since it's easier to slip away if you have that option." Zora paced her living room. "I also heard he's the department chair's nephew. And there's no way Dr. Graham's travel would have been authorized without his approval."

"Okay, I'll go and speak with Dr. Anderson. I'm still at the hospital."

"I'm coming to meet you there."

"No, I don't think that's a good idea. You should stay at home. I don't want them thinking that you are related in any way to my investigation. That would draw more attention to you."

Zora collapsed on the couch and let out a heavy sigh. The inactivity was killing her. "Okay."

"I'll call you back as soon as I'm done, alright?"

"That's fine." She disconnected the call.

With nothing else to do but wait, Zora decided to take a quick shower, after which she ate some cereal for breakfast. As she was wiping the dish to put it away, the black phone rang.

Zora scrambled to pick it up with her free hand. "Hey, Dave."

"You were right. Dr. Anderson authorized Graham's travel, but someone else made the request."

Zora's interest was piqued. "Who did?"

"Dr. Edwards."

The dish slipped from her hand and crashed to the floor.

4

"Zora! Are you okay?" Dave exclaimed from the other end of the line. Zora could hear the sound of a chair crashing to the floor in the background.

She held the edge of the sink with unsteady hands and took a deep breath. "Yes, I'm okay. It was just a plate."

"Are you sure you are alright?"

Zora took more deep breaths. "Yes, I'm fine. I just didn't expect ... Dr. Edwards is my mentor, the one I told you about."

"The one you told about the missing patients."

"Yes. Why would he go out of his way to request for Graham's leave except ...?"

"Except if he was involved in the case as well."

The implications were terrifying. Zora couldn't … didn't want to believe it was true. The only way to be sure was if she heard it directly from the horse's mouth. Zora nestled her phone between her shoulder and her neck and grabbed the broom and dustpan from a corner of the kitchen. "I'm coming to the hospital."

"Zora, I don't think—"

She dropped the broom on the floor next to the plate shards. "I'm on my way, Dave." She ended the call.

Zora slipped the phone into her inner jean pocket, grabbed the broom, and swept up the broken pieces. She dumped them in the garbage can and returned the broom and dustpan to their places.

Picking up her bag from her room, she hurried out of the apartment and down the stairs.

But she didn't make it far before someone grabbed her from behind. The nasty smell of sweaty armpits threatened to choke her, and foul breath fanned her cheek. Zora didn't bother to think. She headbutted whoever was holding her, but it seemed he'd anticipated her move and swung his head away. Zora's head only met empty air, and her eyes spun from the effort.

The man tightened his arms around her neck. Zora found it hard to breathe, and she clawed against the chokehold. But the arms held her steady in an ironclad grip. It was almost like she was an ant trying to move a boulder.

But Zora refused to give up. She bit down hard on his right arm. He flinched and loosened his grip. It was enough for her to take a quick deep inhale as she drove her foot backwards to meet his groin. The man let go and grunted in pain. Zora took off and scrambled down the remaining stairs towards her building's main entrance.

She swung the door open, the smell of freedom a few steps away. But a hand came out of nowhere and clamped a handkerchief reeking of chloroform over her nose. She fought to push the handkerchief away, but it was no use.

Her world dimmed and went black.

35

Zora opened her eyes to find herself in a cavernous room that appeared to be part of a warehouse. Large drums covered in dark-colored stains were piled in the right corner ahead of her. Her head pounded, and her eyes hurt from the light that streamed in through an open window. She tried to raise her hand to shield her eyes and realized she couldn't move it. She looked down and saw that her body, hands, and feet were tied to a chair. Zora tried to shift the chair, but it appeared to be secured to a beam behind her.

"Welcome back, Zora."

Zora turned to the sound of the voice. It was one she knew and had heard so many times. Dr. Edwards loomed over her in a dark blue three-piece suit.

She shook her head to clear it. "Where am I?" she asked.

"It doesn't matter," he said.

Zora's vision cleared. She could now see Dr. Edwards standing next to someone that looked a lot like the person that had bumped into her at the ER entrance, the guy called Thunder. He looked even more ferocious than before.

Zora gasped. She'd suspected as much when Dave told her that Dr. Edwards had requested Graham's vacation, but it was different to see it play out before her eyes. It had been him all along. Dr. Edwards, the very person she'd trusted. Her heart squeezed in pain, and Zora would have doubled over if that was possible.

Her heart raced. She needed to get out of here. No one knew where she was, except … She looked down at her neck.

"It's gone," Dr. Edwards said. "The pendant you wear around your neck? I threw it away. I'd heard about how it had saved your life before. And I couldn't make the mistake of leaving it on you."

Zora's face tightened. The pendant had been a gift from her late father. "You had no right!" she said.

"No need to get all worked up about it. It's not like you are going to need it ever again."

Zora's shoulders fell. Now no one truly knew where

she was. She might just die here. But she wasn't going to stop fighting for her life till her very last breath. She would keep him talking in the meantime while she waited for an opportunity to save herself.

A lump in the corner behind Dr. Edwards and Thunder moved slightly. What was that? The mass shifted again. Zora craned her neck to see, and then realized what she was looking at when she saw the distinct red hair matted around one end of the lump.

"Christina!" Zora cried out. She tried to get up, but the ropes held her back.

Dr. Edwards chuckled. "Don't worry. She's not dead. Yet. I thought it might be best if you died together, best friends and all." Dr. Edwards walked a few steps toward Zora and stopped. His lanky frame blocked any further view of Christina.

Zora's nostrils flared. "How could you? What have you done to her?" she snapped.

Dr. Edwards snickered, a laugh that grated on Zora's nerves. "You've heard the phrase—curiosity kills the cat?" His face twisted in anger. "She should have stayed out of our business!"

Zora leaned away as if struck. This was a side of him that she had never seen. The man behind the friendly mask.

He stooped to Zora's eye level. "Zora," he said, his

voice now back at a normal pitch, "I think you should worry about yourself." He repeatedly jabbed his finger at her. "You couldn't let sleeping dogs lie, could you? Even after I advised you not to report it."

"But how …? How could you be involved in something like this?"

"How could I not, when there was so much money to be made? You would never understand. You with your rich mother and your easy life."

"That's not an excuse." Zora was blessed to have come from a wealthy home, but there were many other doctors who didn't have much, and they'd never done something as vile as this.

"Excuse? Who said anything about an excuse?" Dr. Edwards stood back up and began to pace. Zora cast a quick glance around the room to see if there was anything that could be used as a weapon should she manage to get herself untied. There was nothing. Her heart sank further.

She turned back to Dr. Edwards. He'd stopped pacing and pushed his oval glasses further up his nose. Zora noticed that Thunder watched his every move in silence. "I've had to work hard for everything. EVERY-THING! They tell you how surgeons are supposed to be rich, but nobody ever talks about how that is only true if you don't have any other debts to pay off. Most of us have massive student loans to deal with, and those loans never went away for me, no matter how much I kept paying them off."

"But in a few years, you would have cleared your debts. You are a brilliant surgeon, and you are in high demand even as a speaker at some of the other medical schools. You could have also gone into private practice if you chose."

Dr. Edwards started pacing again. "Have you forgotten that it takes a lot of money to open up a practice of your own? Where would that money have come from? I was drowning in debt so I couldn't qualify for more loans, and on top of that I had a mortgage and a family to take care of. And a few years? That was the one thing I didn't have. My wife was threatening to leave me—I couldn't even make it up to her for never being home from all the long hours I had to put in. Things looked hopeless until these gentlemen came along with a proposal." Dr. Edwards waved his hand to indicate Thunder. "They would make my debts disappear, and I could become a rich man. And all I had to do was use my skills."

"But what about the Hippocratic Oath? The oath you swore to do no harm."

Dr. Edwards stopped walking and stared at her like she'd gone mad. "But I wasn't doing any harm. I was actually giving the patients a better chance to live. You saw how they looked when they arrived at the ER." Zora remembered how sick John Doe and Jasmine had been. "I was only involved in the cleanup. That's all we doctors ever did." By this time, Thunder had moved to Dr. Edwards' side. Zora could smell his unwashed body from where he stood. She struggled not to retch.

She forced herself to take a deep breath. After a moment, her stomach calmed. "But what about the other doctors? Graham? How could they be involved in something like this?"

"They all had needs, and these guys took care of them. You have no idea what it means to worry about money all the time and then have that burden removed. Technically, they did nothing wrong. We never harmed anyone and only cleaned up after the mess."

"So who did the resections?"

Dr. Edwards' mouth thinned into a tight line. He said nothing. Thunder glared at Zora.

Zora had to keep him talking. She tried another question. "What about the anesthesiologist and the scrub nurses? They weren't from Lexinbridge Regional. And who were those patients?"

Thunder whispered something in Dr. Edwards' ear. Zora couldn't hear what he said.

"It doesn't matter," she heard Dr. Edwards say to Thunder. She's going to die anyway."

Zora's heart caught in her throat. She couldn't die now. Her heart beat faster. Maybe she should have stayed home like Dave had advised. But then she might never have seen Christina again. And she needed to save her.

But what if she never saw Dave again? She'd been fighting her feelings with everything that had been going on, but the attraction had increased instead of waning. She needed to know if he felt the same way. And maybe she could take a chance with him despite how terrible her schedule looked. She also hadn't found her sister yet. "Please God, help me," she whispered.

Dr. Edwards chuckled. "Prayer isn't going to help you, my dear." He stuffed his hands into his pants pockets. "You don't need to worry your pretty head about the operating team. The patients, on the other hand, made a choice. Including John Doe and Jasmine."

"So there really was a John Doe!"

"Yes, I chose to deny his existence since it was for your own good. The less you knew, the better off you were."

"I don't agree."

Dr. Edwards ignored her response. "Like I was saying, each of these patients desperately wanted a green card, so they signed a marriage contract— Thunder and his guys would find a US citizen for them to marry to be able to stay permanently in the country in exchange for a kidney. They would pretend to live together since the marriage was strictly contractual and would divorce once they got the green card. Unfortunately, it was at their own risk, but it was a choice they made."

"But Jasmine was so young. There's no way she would have made that choice."

"She came here illegally with her parents, who I heard died later in an accident. They still owed a lot of money to the people who brought them over, and she needed a green card as well. A pity she was pretty, so she had to pay off her family's debt. I hear she tried to run away, so she ended up dead."

Zora was sick with revulsion. This time she couldn't hold back the vomit, and it splattered on her jeans and ran down her leg. Some spittle hung from the corner of her mouth, but she couldn't wipe it off. "How can you live with yourself?"

"Look, they made their choices. If I wasn't there to help, they would have died faster."

Thunder whispered in Dr. Edwards' ear. Dr. Edwards nodded.

"Okay. Time's up for Q&A. My dear Zora, you were so intelligent, and I had high hopes for you. What a pity and a waste. Goodbye." Thunder pulled a gun from his jacket and aimed it at Zora.

"Wait. Hold on. Don't do it!" Zora fought against her restraints to break free, but the ropes were too tight.

A shot rang out.

Zora flinched and shut her eyes, but she felt no pressure or pain. What had happened? She opened her eyes to see Thunder slumped on the floor with a gaping hole on the side of his head. Dr. Edwards was nowhere to be seen.

She heard the sound of running feet and turned her head. Dave raced to her with some other cops behind him.

"Thank goodness. Are you okay?" He quickly untied her hands and legs.

Zora collapsed against him and burst out crying. She was safe and free. It felt good to feel his arms around her.

"Shh… shh…" He rubbed his hand against her back. "It's alright now. You are safe."

Then she remembered. "Christina!" she said,

pointing to the corner of the room where she lay unmoving.

"Get an EMT in here. Now!" Dave called out.

And that was the last thing Zora heard before she blacked out.

36

Zora opened her eyes to see she was lying in a hospital bed. Her whole body ached. She looked around and realized the narrow white-walled room looked familiar.

"Thank God you are finally awake." Brian's worried face came into view.

Zora tried to raise herself, but her limbs felt like they belonged to someone else, and she fell back on the pillows.

"Don't try too hard," Brian said as he helped her sit up.

"What happened?" Zora's voice sounded like an old woman's.

Brian straightened back up once he'd adjusted the

sheets. "They brought you in yesterday. You gave us quite a shock."

Zora closed her eyes briefly as she tried to remember what had happened. The events of yesterday came rushing back to her. She was lucky to be alive.

"You've been out of it for about twenty-four hours," Brian said. "How do you feel now?"

Zora opened her eyes. "Like I was bulldozed with a truck."

Brian chuckled. "That bad?"

Then Zora remembered. "What about Christina?" she asked.

"She is in the ICU. She's regained consciousness, but they want to observe her for another twenty-four hours."

She let out a sigh of relief. "I'm glad she is okay." She tried to get up. "I need to see her."

"Whoa, hold your horses." Brian touched her arm to restrain her. "She's asleep now. You can visit her later."

Zora leaned back on the bed. She was exhausted. She would look in on Christina later.

"Your mom also came by and stayed the night," Brian said.

Zora sat up. "Really?"

"I'm serious. But she worked on her legal briefs the whole time."

Zora laughed and held her side. "Good old Mom. Now, that I'll believe."

"She promised to get another tracker, one more discreet and definitely not a pendant."

Zora touched her neck. "I miss the one I had."

"Sure you do. Maybe you'll find another one you'll love."

"I'm not sure. I think I'll stay without one for a while."

Her hospital phone rang. "I wonder who it is?" Brian said. "The nurses have been very diligent about blocking callers." He reached forward and picked the phone. "Who is this?" He listened for a moment and then turned to Zora. "It's Stewart. Do you want to speak with him?"

Zora gestured for Brian to hand over the phone. "Stewart," she said into the receiver.

"Hi, Dr. Smyth. I heard what happened and just called to find out how you are doing," Stewart said.

"I'm good. Thanks for asking."

"I'm sorry to hear about Dr. Edwards. Who would have thought?"

Zora said nothing. Dr. Edwards had been a good

mentor to her, as much as she despised what he had done.

"Have you heard anything else?"

"No. But I have a question for you. Why did you lie to me about John Doe?"

"John Doe?"

"You said you never knew the patient, but now we know he really was a patient here."

"I'm sorry about that. I couldn't afford to tell the truth. After you left, I got a call from my girlfriend that she was in town and waiting for me at the hospital entrance. I hadn't seen her face-to-face in like three months, and I ended up spending some time with her. By the time I got back, John Doe was missing, and I was afraid that I would be blamed for it. As a lowly junior surgical resident with no connections, I could be expelled from the program. So I chose to deny instead. I'm sorry."

Zora didn't know what to say. He had made her look like a fool. He needed a good talking to, but today wasn't the right time. She was too tired to even think.

"Dr. Smyth, I hope I didn't take too much of your time," Stewart said. "I just called to make sure you are okay."

"Thanks." Zora placed the phone back on its cradle and lowered herself back on the pillows.

"What did he want?" Brian asked.

"He just called to find out how I'm doing. He helped me search for Christina when I was first looking for her and knew about one of the missing patients."

"Strange little fella. Too smooth if you ask me. Are you sure he doesn't have a crush on you?"

Zora laughed, and her body ached from the effort. "Brian, cut it out!" She stretched out her hand to swat him, but he moved beyond her reach. Brian chuckled.

"By the way, I like your new beau," he said.

Zora's head snapped up. "What?"

"You know, the handsome detective. He stayed with you all night and only left this morning. He said he'd be back later."

Zora felt her face flush with heat.

"He's not my beau," she mumbled.

"Oooh, you are blushing. I've never seen you blush."

"Brian, cut it out," Zora warned him.

"Cut what out?" Dave said as he strode into the hospital room.

Zora wished the bed could swallow her. She tried to sink in deeper, but couldn't help peeking at Dave at the same time. He looked so handsome in his light grey button-down shirt and jeans.

"She was just—" Brian started.

"Brian!"

"Okay, okay," Brian held up his hands in mock surrender. "I'll just go and leave you two lovebirds alone." He winked at Zora.

Zora grabbed her pillow and threw it at Brian's head. It fell short, and Brian left the room laughing.

Dave walked to the side of her bed and sat down on the edge. "How are you feeling?"

Zora's face felt impossibly hot and she squirmed. "Much better. Thanks for saving me. I mean us. How did you find me at the warehouse? I thought all hope was lost when I found out my pendant was gone."

"I didn't even know your pendant could track your location until Brian told me after you were admitted. I had put a tracker in the burner phone I gave you. So when I called repeatedly and you didn't answer, I feared the worst and activated the tracker. I'm glad we got there on time."

Zora sighed in relief. "I'm glad too. I had tucked the phone into my inner jean pocket, which was probably the only reason they didn't find it on me. And I'm sure they didn't expect me to have another phone beyond the one in my bag. Speaking of bags, where's mine?"

"It's at the police station as evidence, but I'm picking it up tomorrow once they've finished with it."

"Thanks. Did you find Dr. Edwards?"

"Oh, we caught him alright, trying to run away. He'd scurried out through a side door at the warehouse that was not really visible unless you knew it was there. But he didn't know our guys had surrounded the warehouse. When he realized it was all over, he sang like a bird and cut a deal. So we got the names of the OR team, and found a judge to issue warrants for their arrests. But we don't know yet if those names are real or fake. Dr. Edwards claimed Thunder was his primary contact with the cartel, though another number had called him once. We ran a trace on the number, but it seems to be unregistered." Dave tucked an errant lock of her hair behind her ear.

For Zora, it felt intimate, a feeling she welcomed. She gave him a small smile.

"He was arraigned this morning," Dave continued. "Bail was set at one million dollars, which his wife paid." "He has been advised to stay in town, and we've added him to the no-flight list. Unfortunately, Thunder died on the spot, so we couldn't get any information from him. We were able to triangulate his home from the calls on his phone, but we searched it and found nothing. It's a dead end."

Zora could see the tension on Dave's face. She wished she could ease his frustration.

"But we'll keep searching. The good thing is that Jasmine's case has been reopened." Dave rearranged the sheets around her. "Two detectives will be coming by later to take your statement with regards to the case. I have to be back at the station then, but I'm sure you'll be fine. They are guys I trust." Dave took her hand and held it in his. "It's been an ordeal, right?" he said softly.

Zora nestled back into the pillows as the warmth from his words wrapped around her. She was just glad to be alive and was grateful that it was all over.

But there was only one place she wished to be. "I want to go home."

EPILOGUE

A week later, Zora was preparing lunch at home. She hummed as she moved about the kitchen in her white tank top and grey capri pants. This was her last day before going back to work, and she'd wanted to cook a thank-you meal for Dave. Well, that was what she called it.

Christina had improved in the following days after being hospitalized, and Zora had gone to see her. They had hugged and cried and cried some more. Christina had taken a month off work and had then travelled home to recuperate at her mom's place. Zora was glad that she hadn't told Christina's mom about what happened. It was now up to Christina to determine how much she got to know.

Christina had explained that she had been

kidnapped after she'd followed the two men she had caught wheeling Jasmine from the SICU. Once she'd come to, she'd found herself in a strange warehouse, tried to send a message to Zora, but had been beaten once they'd realized she'd sent them on a wild goose chase. That was probably when her necklace broke— the same one that Zora had found on the floor of Christina's room. She'd been confident that Zora would understand what had happened once she saw her trashed room, though her panic toy idea hadn't worked.

Lexinbridge Regional Hospital's ad hoc disciplinary committee had reversed its decision and lifted her suspension once the case broke, and MEC had accepted the recommendation. Dr. Anderson had resigned, and another department chair had temporarily taken his place. Zora heard from Dave that Graham had fled to Dubai from London to avoid extradition back to the US.

The mystery OR team was still at large. They had disappeared without a trace. Dave had confirmed there was no Dr. Latam licensed to practice medicine in the state or board-certified with the American Board of Anesthesiology—it had been a fake name. The police was trying to track down anyone that fit the description Zora and Christina had given the sketch artist about him, but it didn't look promising. Dave was also leading the investigation into the cartel that was behind the illegal organ harvesting business.

The SICU nurse had finally surfaced; she had been on a much-needed cruise vacation to Antigua, which was why she had switched off her phone. Her statement corroborated what Christina had already told the detectives.

All in all, Zora had gotten her career back. But it would take some time before everything returned to normal.

The oven chimed. Zora opened its door, pulled the tray filled with grilled salmon cuts, and set it on the kitchen countertop. She grinned. Good thing she hadn't burned them. It would have been a terrible first impression to give Dave of her cooking. Her nose tingled as the heady smell of spices filled the air. Now all she had left to do was mix the salad ingredients in the glass bowl and cover it up.

Her doorbell rang. Zora set the salad spoon on the counter and hurried to the door. She opened it, expecting to see Dave. Instead she recognized Dave's partner and another guy.

"What are you doing here?" she asked him.

"Dr. Smyth, you are under arrest for the murder of Dr. Edwards."

The man in the car watched as Zora was led by the detectives into the police car. The doors slammed shut, and the car drove off. It was a pity that she had to be the fall guy. She should have stopped her friend Dave from digging into the man's profitable organ business, one that he planned to continue even though his partner, Drake Pierce, was dead.

Since the case had broken open, he'd sent his boys to clean out the penthouse, even Drake's body. Unfortunately, it had been too late to harvest Drake's organs. His father had filed a missing person's report on his behalf, but the man was sure he was only too happy to have his company back. The old man was cold that way.

It was time to leave and get ready for work. The man pressed the ignition button, and his car roared to life. He nudged the car into the street and drove away, his ID badge swinging from side to side as it hung from the rear-view mirror.

The ID card with the name Thomas Stewart.

Thank you so much for reading!

Want to know what happens next to Dr. Zora Smyth? Sign up now at dobicross.com.

If you've loved reading LETHAL INCISION, Dobi would be grateful if you could spend a few minutes to leave a review (as short as you like) on the book's Amazon page. Your review would help bring it to the attention of other readers. Thank you very much.

Check out all Dobi Cross books at smarturl.it/DobiCross.

ACKNOWLEDGMENTS

Writing a book is harder and more rewarding than I could have ever imagined. And it would not have been possible without the support, love, and encouragement from my number one cheerleader, my dearest mom. My life would never have been this awesome and wonderful without you.

Of course, I have to thank my precious little DC for his smiles and antics. You brighten my day and give me the strength to keep pushing through.

Thank you to my sisters for encouraging me on this wonderful journey. And a special thanks to my baby brother (who is so not a baby anymore) for being super supportive and checking in on my progress. You guys are the best.

Thank you to my wonderful author friends. You

know who you are. Your selflessness and willingness to share what you know has made my writing journey smoother and an exciting one. And a special thanks to my ARC team whose support have made a difference.

Most of all, I want to thank God who gave me life, surrounded me with the most wonderful people, and loved me all the way. You make my life complete.

And finally, a special thanks to all my readers whose love of my stories spur me on to write more.

Thank you!

ABOUT THE AUTHOR

As a former physician and business executive in another life, Dobi Cross loves to write thrilling stories with heart. Whether it'd be medical thrillers, or whatever book that takes her fancy, Dobi Cross loves to dream up and pen everyday characters that rise above unfavorable circumstances to overcome incredible odds.

Lethal Incision is the second book in the Zora Smyth Medical Thriller Series. Sign up at dobicross.com to be notified when the next Dr. Zora Smyth Book comes out!

Thanks for reading LETHAL INCISION!
www.dobicross.com
hello@dobicross.com
facebook.com/dobicrossauthor
bookbub.com/profile/dobi-cross

Made in the USA
Las Vegas, NV
26 April 2021